ECHOES OF LOVE

By the Author

The Set Piece

Heartwood

Tread Lightly

Romancing the Kicker

Lean in to Love

Echoes of Love

Visit us at www.boldstrokesbooks.com

ECHOES OF LOVE

by
Catherine Lane

2025

ECHOES OF LOVE

ISBN 13: 978-1-63679-835-6

This Trade Paperback Original Is Published By
Bold Strokes Books, Inc.
P.O. Box 249
Valley Falls, NY 12185

First Edition: September 2025

Credits
Editor: Barbara Ann Wright
Production Design: Stacia Seaman
Cover Design by Tammy Seidick

Acknowledgments

First and foremost, my deepest thanks to my publisher—Radclyffe, Sandy, Ruth, Cindy, and everyone at Bold Strokes Books. Your grace, professionalism, and unwavering support make it a joy to work both with you and for you. I know just how fortunate I am to be part of this incredible publishing family.

To my brilliant editor, Barbara Ann Wright—thank you for making me a better writer with every book. Working through edits with you has become one of my favorite parts of the writing process. Your insight and encouragement are invaluable.

Heartfelt thanks to my trusted beta readers, Liz Hayden and Ann Etter. Your honesty, kindness, and thoughtful feedback have helped shape this book in all the best ways. Liz, you've supported me since we lived on Spruce Street, and your belief in me from day one has meant more than I can ever express.

I owe a special debt of gratitude to my physics consultants. Robbie Kresch, thank you for generously offering ideas and solutions—and for patiently explaining them again when I lost the thread. And to my son, who has always claimed to "know things"—turns out, he does. Your explanation of how energy is grounded not only informed the story but grounded me, too.

Finally, to my wife—my greatest supporter and biggest fan—I love you.

To Pam: Thank you for all your support
and for introducing me to your friends.

Chapter One

The Present: Hazel

Where the hell was Cherry?

The phone rang in the main gallery for the fourth time, then rolled over into my workspace in the back when no one answered. Was the gallery so busy that Cherry couldn't answer? Seriously, that was practically her only job.

I almost didn't answer the phone. I was being petty, sitting in the back office of the gallery, digging my nails into my palms. *Shit.* Hiring Cherry had been a colossal mistake. Stupidly—or maybe it was plain cowardice—I hadn't said anything to my business partner, Keera, at the time. Now I was stuck doing both our jobs.

I should've let it go to voice mail. Proof of Cherry's actual incompetence might have come in handy, but I hated loose ends. So I picked up. "Hazel Ross Gallery." Even I heard the annoyance in my voice, so I tried to soften it. "May I help you?"

"I hope so." The woman ran her words together quickly. "I'm looking for Hazel Ross."

I winced. "I'm sorry, she's not available. Can I take a message?" Total cop-out, I know. I was Hazel Ross of the Hazel Ross Gallery, but I was more interested in edging out of my office to see why Cherry couldn't pick up the damn phone.

"Oh no. Are you sure?" The caller's voice cracked in frustration. "Ann Ross suggested I call her. That's her grandmother. She even gave me her cell phone information, but I can't find it. It's an emergency."

Shit, shit. I froze halfway into the hallway. It was one of *those* calls. I'd told Gran a million times to stop giving out my number to anyone who had *unexplainable problems.*

Sometimes, I saw reflections of the past like little movies that randomly popped up right in front of me. Not ghosts, not visions, just echoes of events that were tied to the location where they originally happened. I had no control over when or where they arrived, and they drove me crazy.

Gran believed it was my civic duty to help anyone in need, and while I was all for paying it forward, most of these people wanted a reality show experience, not the unexamined truth.

Shit, shit, shit. If Gran had given out my cell phone, she was asking for the favor, and I would do absolutely anything for her. "Sorry." I sighed. "This is Hazel Ross. I thought you were a gallery customer."

"Oh, thank goodness." Relief poured out of the phone. "Look, Hazel, we're in trouble up here. Terrible trouble. I've no idea what is going on." She began to trip over her words again. "But it's getting worse. Jo and I are beyond frustrated, and the dog won't even come into the house. I can't—"

"Lauren? You didn't call her, did you?" Another voice cut in from the background. I must have been on speakerphone. "I thought we agreed. We weren't going to get her involved." This woman's voice was low and calm, with a hint of a storm brewing.

And really sexy.

"She can help, Jo."

"You're being ridiculous."

"I told you. Grandmother said to call her," Lauren shot back. "She can put this to rest once and for all. She can communicate with whatever is here."

"No, I can't," I jumped in, trying to end this fast. "There are no such things as ghosts."

"See?" Jo said, her voice getting closer. "We don't always have to do what Grandmother tells us. Besides, those ghost hunting shows on TV are made up."

"She's right," I said again. "And for the record, I am not a ghost hunter. I'm a photographer, and I—"

The phone shifted, and Jo's voice, smooth and intense, was right in my ear. "Ms. Ross, is it?"

I swallowed hard. I'd been single way too long. "Yes?"

"I'm sorry my cousin bothered you. She's a little…excitable, but we don't need your help. Thank you for your time. And please thank your grandmother too. Good-bye."

The line went dead. I quickly shook off whatever fantasy was materializing around Jo. One problem solved, and I barely had to lift a finger. But problem number two? I moved into the main gallery.

Problem number two was standing in the middle of the room glued to her phone.

Cherry.

She was dressed...well, *casual* didn't even begin to cover it. Shorts so tiny, the pockets stuck out and a frilly crop top that barely skimmed her belly. Not exactly work appropriate.

I headed over. "Cherry?"

She didn't look up. "Hold up," she muttered, her thumbs flying over the phone.

"I need you to answer the gallery phone when it rings," I said firmly.

"Keera said I could take a break every hour," she replied, still staring at her screen. "And she's the boss."

"She's only half the boss," I corrected. "And you're looking at the other half. Well, you would be if you put your phone away." Too many words; I'd lost her. The gallery phone rang again. "Break's over," I said simply.

Cherry shot me a death glare but dragged herself over to the desk. She didn't put her cell away, and new texts dinged with almost every step. At least she dropped it on the table to answer the gallery phone.

"Hazel Ross Gallery." Cherry listened, rolling her eyes like doing her job was the biggest inconvenience of her life. "Yeah, it's on till the end of the month." Her lips pressed into a tight slash. "Yeah, you'll see the GloFish as soon as you walk in." She paused, scanning the room for a quick exit. "Yeah, Suki Lush is in some of the photos. Oh, is there any chance you can call back later?" Her whole face lit up as she dropped the phone into its headset, cutting off the call.

I followed her gaze to the front door, and honestly, my breath quickened as well.

Keera swept into the gallery like she owned the place, which, to be fair, she half did. She was tall, red-haired, and gorgeous in a white-on-white pantsuit with no shirt underneath. The jacket, open to almost her belly button, showed enough cleavage to bring women, men, even aliens into her orbit.

Keera was my current gallery partner and ex-girlfriend. A fifty-fifty split in the business that I had stupidly agreed to after a night of mind-blowing sex. On my end. In hindsight, going down on me twice had probably been a surefire strategy to soften me up for the negotiations later. We'd already been together for over a year, and I'd thought she was the one.

We'd met at a bar. I was celebrating my graduation from California College of the Arts in Oakland, and she, bored and beautiful, had taken me home for some "low-stakes fun." After several orgasms on her end, I'd showed her a picture of my childhood dog that was tucked away in my wallet, and everything shifted. She had studied it and given me the first true smile of the night.

"How did you get it to look like that?" she had asked.

"Like what?" I'd never thought of it as anything more than a clumsy photo of a dog I loved.

"Like it knows you're taking the picture. Like it's completely opening up to you. This is incredible, Hazel."

I'd wanted to correct her: no dog was ever an *it*. But a deep flush had crept across my cheeks, and I hadn't wanted to ruin what might have been developing because she had seemed interested in more than low-stakes fun.

"I thought you said you took pictures of still life and architecture."

I'd nodded. I had all the way through art school. I'd already seen too many people in real life and in my reflections.

"Could you do this again? Say, with another dog or any animal?"

"Yes." I would've told her I could've photographed an alien on Mars. All I'd wanted was another night with her.

Keera had cupped my cheek. I hadn't realized then that it was her one tender gesture. "Okay."

She could see I had a gift, not that I saw reflections of the past as large as life. That confession came later, and truth be told, she'd never believed a word of it. No, she had seen it from a different angle. My ability to capture something emotional in my photographs. She could already see a million pictures: all animal portraits that connected with people in a deeply human way.

To her credit, she had been the first person to believe in my talent. She had swept me into her orbit, and together, we'd built everything: studio sessions with celebrities who had money to burn, a lucrative art gallery, and an impressive online presence.

Then she'd dumped me.

Only personally. Professionally, we were still very much an item. But I was no longer the one she called to her bed. Cherry had that privilege now. With way too much ass hanging out of her shorts, she walked up to Keera and kissed her noisily on the lips.

"Hey, babe." Keera kept the kiss short. "I need to talk to Hazel. Dinner when you get off?"

She didn't wait for a response and held out to me the *People* magazine that had been tucked under her arm. "Got an advance copy. The article's fantastic, if I do say so myself. Come take a look." She walked away just far enough to make it clear I was supposed to follow. I did. Like always.

My office was more functional than flashy, mostly a workroom. A large butcher block with lots of drawers for flat files sat in the middle of the room. Bright red barstools gave the room comfortable seating and a pop of color. An L-shaped desk with four huge monitors took over one corner, and the rest of the room was cabinet storage for my equipment. Pretty bare-bones since most of my shoots were on location, and if we did need a studio, Keera rented one down the street from the San Francisco Museum of Modern Art.

She dropped the magazine on the butcher block and pulled two stools together so we could both look at it. "Page thirty-six." She slid the magazine across the smooth wood as if she was giving me control.

I flipped the pages slowly, already dreading what I might see. Keera had been pushing my brand in a direction I wasn't sure about. And when I hit page thirty-six, I knew for sure. I hated it. Big, bold black letters summed up the artist I'd become:

Hazel Ross

Pet Photographer to the Stars

A touched-up version of myself stared at me from under the title. My eyes, normally a washed-out blue, were now the azure of a Caribbean sea. My curly, shoulder-length hair was a little blonder and a lot tamer. My teeth, without me accompanying them, had been to several whitening sessions with a dentist. Finally, the scar on my forehead, thanks to a skiing accident in Tahoe, had completely vanished.

"What the fuck?"

"What part?"

"All of it. The picture is ridiculous." I squinted. "Did they give me lipstick?"

"Maybe a touch. You look fantastic. It's great marketing."

"And who the hell came up with this?" I jabbed my forefinger at the headline. "Pet Photographer to the Stars?"

"I did."

"It's not true."

"It is."

"Well, I don't want it to be true."

"You're the only one." Keera shot back. "People eat this stuff up,

Hazel. They come to the gallery to see the celebrity pics and then buy prints and T-shirts by the boatload."

"I know how it works, Keera." I was annoyed but maybe because I could still see her hand cupped around Cherry's cheek.

The true headline should've been:

U-Hauled or U-Stalled

Hazel Ross Can't Get Her Ex Out of Her Head

Keera tapped the top of the page like she was sealing the deal. "This pays for your new-build condo with views of both bridges. It pays the monthly stipend to your grandmother, and it writes all those checks to more animal charities than I can count."

"I know." I dropped my head in defeat. She had me beat. We both had a hand in creating the ridiculous Hazel Ross grinning up at me. "Tell them to get rid of the lipstick."

"Okay. I'll ask. Would you read the article, though? It's good."

"Fine." I pulled the magazine to me.

She wasn't wrong. The staff writer had painted a broader picture of me as an artist. She did start with the celebrity shoots to hook the reader. Some of the most famous appeared with their wolf-hybrid dogs and Savannah cats, cobras and pot-bellied pigs. But soon, the article shifted to me. How my photographs without celebrities had also appeared in *National Geographic* and *Life* and how they depicted the magic and vulnerability of animals in the wild. She even credited my *Animals Lost in Nature* series with advancing environmental conservation efforts. And Keera was right, the manatee and dolphin photos at the end would fund even more charity donations. Damn her.

Then I remembered I had another bone to pick with her. "I'm not sure Cherry's working out."

Her smile tightened. "Excuse me?"

"She's unprofessional. She dresses like a teenager who's going clubbing. The calls roll back here so often, I can't get my work done. And today, the one call I heard her answer, she hung up the second you walked through the door."

A tiny, self-satisfied gleam hit Keera's eyes. Cherry's loyalty wasn't just noted. It was rewarded. "She wouldn't want me to tell you this, but she's having a real problem with her roommate, and she may have to find a new living situation. We both need to be sensitive to her situation."

"What you mean is that I need to be more sensitive," I snapped. "You can't have it both ways. We need to protect this business, and you can't hire whoever you're sleeping with." What I didn't add was that it wasn't good for my mental health either. I didn't need to see the endless parade of women, all way sexier than I was, who had taken my place.

Keera stood in deliberate silence, pulled the magazine to her, and dropped it into her oversized purse.

I bit my lip. Shit. Had I gone too far?

"We can talk about it when we get back," she said in a tactical shift, her retreat smooth.

I didn't want to, but I bit. "From where?"

"New York. Great news. I didn't want to tell you until it was settled, but I've been talking to Caleb Fisher's manager. You know he had that drunken debacle in some nightclub after one of his concerts, and they're looking to humanize him. They got *Vogue* to agree to a spread, and he told them that he wanted to be photographed with his falcon and hawk. He saw the shoot we did for Suki, and it's practically a done deal."

This was Keera at her best. She ran from a negative to a positive so quickly, it swept the argument off its feet. And truth be told, it had always worked on me.

Thankfully, my cell phone on the butcher block dinged, and in true Cherry style, I turned the phone toward me.

Schlosschen Meerblick, 1 Steward Lane, Cypress Shores CA, Lauren.

So she hadn't lost my contact info after all.

"Hazel, are you listening? I negotiated the copyright on two prints. This will set a new bar for all our future contracts." That self-satisfied gleam was back in her eyes. "You want an aisle or a window seat?"

My phone dinged again. *Please, please come. Help us.*

I said nothing. Keera could keep Cherry for now, but I wasn't going to stay and watch them slip out, hand in hand, to their romantic dinner. Instead, I grabbed my phone and a full camera bag that I always had ready for quick departures.

"We can talk about it when I get back." I emphasized the *I* as if I was the one with all the control.

"What? Where are you going?" Her voice rose in pitch with each word.

I didn't bother to answer. She'd literally and psychologically turn me around if I stayed.

On my way! I texted back to Lauren. I was locked in now. I only hoped I wasn't jumping from the pan right into the fire.

THE LETTERS

The Past: Eliza

March 1, 1925

Dear Joelyn,

Thank you so much for lowering your standards and playing tennis with me today at the Woman's Athletic Club. It couldn't have been much fun since I can barely lob the ball over the net. You, as club champion, are surely used to more exciting matches. Would you believe, though, I had a ball? The way you turned every shot into a game and all your clever jests. I dare say you were entertaining yourself as well. Is everything always so much fun with you?

I must apologize for Mother's behavior. Surely you noticed how Mother, who shames me almost daily by trying to climb into the city's elite social salons, is actively courting your family and the Steward name. I hope you do not have a bruise from where she strong-armed you into a match with me. Your graciousness on and off the court is much appreciated.

Yours most truly,
Elizabeth Hamwell
The Durham House
Pacific Heights

❖

March 7, 1925

Dear Joelyn,

Our second tennis match yesterday was such a delight. Swell for me, at least. I am sure you have a better use for your time. Be aware that Mother is counting on your proper upbringing to keep you from refusing her. Do tell her that you are swamped when she accosts you at the club again. Mention one of your mother's salon parties and how you must help with the arrangements. Tell her of Mark Twain or some nifty jazz musician who will be there. Mother will be so frozen with jealousy that you can slip away while she's picking her jaw up off the floor. Seriously, Mother is obsessed with getting into the Social Register and Record. Since Father's name or his hard-earned grocery money doesn't automatically open those doors, she needs, as you know, five enthusiastic sponsors. She already has Mrs. Davidson. I shudder to think how. Mrs. Littney and Mrs. Karlton are dragging their heels, waiting until one of the darlings of San Francisco society gives their blessing before they throw in their support. Mother thinks that your family with your liberal politics and your bohemian soirées is her best chance.

Oh my! Please do not take this letter as my joining her campaign. It's meant as a warning. She spins a web that is very hard to escape. I am not sure why I write you all this. You were there, of course. Usually, I am quite shy, but I feel very at ease with you, and I like our new connection.

Sincerely,
Elizabeth Hamwell
The Durham House
Pacific Heights

March 20, 1925

Dear Joelyn,

What a treat to receive your letter, and thank you for understanding Father's telephone prohibition. You should have seen Mother's face when I flashed your letter and whisked myself upstairs without a word. She was positively beside herself, which has been the only good ever to come of Father's silly rule. He insists that proper young ladies do not use the telephone. But between us, it's more than his controlling nature. It's fear. When he was a little boy, supposedly someone he knew, a distant relative, was struck by lightning while talking on the phone during a storm. He said it scarred him for life, and even now, he conducts most of his business correspondence by letter and messenger.

The American Telephone and Telegraph advertisement with Aladdin's genie hasn't helped either. You know the one where the genie has his hands up and looks as if he is casting a spell on both you and the telephone? He might have been softening to an occasional call, but now with that slogan, "Everyday Magic," he knows that something sinister is afoot.

It drives my beau, Henry, absolutely batty. He's swell about it, mostly. Father insists that we arrange our outings by calling cards like it's still the 1800s. They come without an envelope, so everyone, including the servants, can peek at them before they reach my room. It's Father's way of keeping tabs, naturally.

You'd like Henry. He's keen on the trumpet and plays in a jazz band. He loves baseball and exploring the art galleries downtown. Between us, we are mostly good friends, a secret I'll keep from my parents since they get hot under the collar whenever he comes calling. You see, his family works for our family, which makes him socially unacceptable to Father, who's forever fretting about what society thinks. They only tolerate Henry because Father is convinced I am far too young to fall in love. In the Hamwell family, we marry old and carefully. Father is certain he'll have plenty of time to impose his will over mine. In fact, when the time comes to marry, he tells me that he will have more say in it than I will. We will see about that.

Your mother's party for the museum sounds so ritzy and exciting. You made the whole night come alive in your letter. I felt like I was there myself. Did you really have champagne? How deliciously scandalous. Father, of course, wouldn't let me near giggle water even before Prohibition. Now that the city is supposedly dry, I may never get my first taste. Oh, horse feathers, Mother is calling. See you soon, I hope.

Yours truly,
Elizabeth
The Durham House
Pacific Heights

CHAPTER TWO

The Present: Hazel

After Keera's and my argument, I burst out of the gallery doors like I was surfacing from deep water. I didn't look back, but I could picture the look on her face as if I held a photo: mouth open, eyes narrowing, her expression both sour and surprised. Other than pure artistic decisions, I rarely said "no" to her, and when I did, it was followed with a quick "I'm so sorry" or "I'll totally make it up to you." But not this time. I walked away without a word. So childish, and boy, did it feel good.

San Francisco was having one of those postcard perfect days, so bright and sunny that the fog and bone-deep chill were a distant memory. I stood on the sidewalk letting the sunshine wash over me, enjoying my sudden freedom. Maybe I was also waiting to see if Keera would come rushing out, arms outstretched, begging me to come back.

She didn't. I'd backed myself into this corner. The only thing I had left to do was punch Lauren's address into my phone's GPS.

I laughed when the map loaded. Of course Cypress Shores was over one hundred miles and two and a half hours away. I'd committed the entire morning to driving up Highway 1, a winding road that always made me carsick. But I'd made my dramatic exit, and pride was a hell of a motivator.

At first, the drive was as good as a therapy session. Open communication with Keera and fresh, ironclad contracts marched through my mind. I could afford a good lawyer now, and for twenty-five miles, I even designed a sleek, modern studio space away from the gallery that was all mine. I'd dump these stupid celebrity contracts and dive into work that had real depth, something edgier that would land me on the cover of *Aperture*, not *People*. My photos had been so flat lately, technically perfect but hollow at the center. Like me?

These fantasies were full of excellent coffee from an all-female roastery next door and clients who appreciated my talent, not just theirs. For a while, I told myself I was manifesting a new future, bringing it into existence with my thoughts. Then, of course, I got stuck behind a lumbering RV crawling up the road, and the cracks began to show.

Even in my imagined dream life, Keera was there. She breezed in with fresh coffee or brought me *Aperture*, asking me to sign the cover for a charity raffle. Even in my escapist fantasies, I couldn't escape her.

I sighed heavily and turned down the volume of my playlist. *Fuck me.* Did I want to get back together with her? All she had to do was waltz in the door, and my whole body responded like a compass finding north. Enough. I couldn't keep doing this.

"Call Gran," I told my phone. "Guess where I'm going," I said when she picked up.

"You're getting those great sandwiches with the garlic sauce from that place in south San Francisco."

"No, but we should totally go there soon." Both Gran and I made a lot of decisions based on our stomachs. We called it our gut instincts.

"Dang, I've been hankering after those sandwiches."

"This might make you even happier. I'm going up to Cypress Shores to see Lauren."

"Who?"

My forehead creased. Was I being conned? These kinds of people found me in all sorts of ways. "I don't know her last name," I confessed. "She said she knew you."

"Oh, you mean Jeannie Steward's granddaughter. They call her Ren." She laughed at herself. "Jeannie and I play mahjong together on Thursdays at the library. It's supposed to improve your cognitive functioning, but honestly, we go to gossip."

"So what did you tell her?" I asked, hoping that it had been a private conversation and that I wasn't going to get phone calls from a dozen grandchildren.

"The usual. You know, that sometimes you can see things or memories that happened long ago. I told her that they weren't alive. Pieces of the past. But I told her that often, you see lost information that can bring closure to situations or give people insight into what might have shaped them. Jeannie didn't seem that interested. I'm surprised she passed it on to Lauren…" She trailed off, trying to emphasize her regret.

"Well, she did," I said accepting her apology. "And now Lauren, like all of these people, is expecting more than I can give her."

"You'll figure out a way to help them, honey. You always do. Thanks so much for doing this."

"Gran, I...I..." The words died in my throat. I couldn't say that this new me included leaving my gift behind and that she couldn't volunteer my services anymore.

"I appreciate the favor. Go up there to see what it's all about."

I could hear her smile all the way up the coast. And maybe that was enough.

"I hear both her grandkids are good people," she added after a beat. "And the house is supposed to be spectacular. It was built in 1895. Jeannie's one of Claude Steward's descendants."

A flicker of excitement rose in me. The Stewards, San Francisco royalty for centuries, had properties up and down the coast. Maybe this wouldn't be a completely wasted trip after all. I loved old houses, and I did have a camera in the trunk.

We chatted until my GPS nudged me off the highway, steering me into the Cypress Shores community.

"Hazel Ross." I held up my driver's license to the guard at the gatehouse.

He scanned the computer in front of him and hit a button to open the gate. "Welcome, Ms. Ross. Follow this road to Meerblick House." He pointed to the eco-friendly graveled road in front of me.

"Thanks," I said and drove into a different world.

Thick, wild coastal meadows stretched as far as I could see, lush and untamed, swaying in the wind. A cluster of modern, timber frame houses, their weathered siding blending naturally with the scenery, dotted the landscape. Walking trails wove between the houses, linking public spaces where a family of deer strolled through the tall grass. The road took me toward the ocean, and when I passed a thicket of twisted cypress trees, like a portal into a fairy land, Meerblick house appeared.

I sucked in a breath. *Holy moly.*

It stood apart from the other homes both in space and design. Neoclassical in style, it looked like something a Greek god might have dropped on the California coast: tall columns, ornate pediments, and windows that stretched to the sky.

"Wow," I whispered, stepping out of the car to stare. Gran was right. Totally worth the drive.

A shadow shifted on the wide porch. It darted toward me, swift and dark. My breath hitched, and I took an automatic step back, my heart racing.

Then two warm paws found my waist, and a wet nose nudged my hand. Jesus, it was a dog.

"Hey, pup. You scared me." I bent to his level and pulled his curly head into my chest. Dogs had always appreciated me, and happily, this wasn't the first dog who had thrown him or herself into my arms. I twisted the collar, looking for a tag and a name.

"Edgar, get down," Lauren called. Even without seeing her, I recognized her voice and looked up to see two women standing on the huge front porch. If one was Lauren, then the other must have been Jo. Cousins, right? But they couldn't have been more different. One was shortish and crackled with the energy of a summer storm. The other was taller, with similar dark hair and a tight, athletic build that hinted at strength and agility. Even standing motionless, there was a grace and ease to her stillness, a readiness that already embraced movement.

"It's okay. I love dogs," I said, looking back and forth between them, hoping for a clue to their identities. There was no way that the lovely voice I heard on the phone belonged to all that grace. No one was that lucky.

"Good. I'm training him not to jump. It's going well, as you can see." I guess she was that lucky. Jo's voice in person was even more musical than over the phone.

She moved effortlessly down the stairs. Her hand barely brushed the banister, not for support but in a gentle acknowledgment of its presence. She raised that same hand to me and confirmed what I already knew. "Hi, I'm Jo."

"Hazel." I stood to shake her hand.

At first, her grip was perfunctory, polite without any real warmth. Then, almost by accident, I glanced up and met her eyes. They were a golden brown, so rich I wondered if the color would spill from them like honey.

As we held each other's gaze, something shifted. The tightness in her jaw softened, and the corners of her lips twitched upward ever so slightly. For the first time in years, my chest tightened with a woman's touch that wasn't Keera's. The sensation was thrilling and terrifying at the same time.

Eventually, I dropped my hand, and Edgar, ready for me, nudged it with his nose. He was one of those puffy designer dogs who was sure everyone loved him. I was more of a "get your dog at the pound" kind of woman, but Edgar's eagerness was so endearing, and my heart went out to him. Besides, my hand in his black and white curls was much safer than lingering in Jo's touch.

Okay, I admitted it, there was totally a vibe between us. It felt good, uplifting even, to be a few feet from her. The reaction surprised me, especially since the ride up here had reminded me how connected to Keera I still was. There had been a few women since our breakup, but most had said I worked too hard or wasn't emotionally available. The truth was that Keera's reflection loomed large in any new relationship. Although strangely, she didn't feel so big right now.

"I'm Lauren." The other woman bounced down the stairs into a second handshake. "Thank you so much for coming." She clasped my hand in both of hers and squeezed energetically. Her brown eyes, so much like Jo's, sparkled with delight, as if meeting me was a real highlight. "I can't wait to see what you're going to find."

Jo tugged on her cousin's arm as if to pull her back to a reasonable reaction, and she said to me, "Look, I'm sorry she dragged you all the way up here. With all due respect to everyone involved, your grandmother, my grandmother, the three of us, this is a colossal waste of time."

Lauren seemed to have other thoughts. She edged around my car and popped the trunk. Looking into its depths, she slowly shook her head. "Is this it? Where's all your stuff?"

"Lauren, what are you doing?" Jo rushed to her side.

"There's nothing in here." She frowned. "Where's your EMF meter and temperature gauge? Or the EVP recorder?"

I joined them and looked into the recesses of the trunk. My camera bag and a small overnight backpack I kept for unforeseen circumstances like this lay in the center. It looked like everything to me. "EVP recorder?" I asked.

"Yeah, the electronic voice phenomenon. How else do you hear what the ghosts are saying? Is it in there?" She pointed to the camera bag, moving ahead at a million miles a minute.

"No, that's my camera." I swallowed, gathering my thoughts before I spoke. "I'm not sure what your grandmother told you, but I hope you heard me on the phone. I'm not a ghost hunter. I don't believe in ghosts."

Jo blew out a breath in relief, but Lauren's whole body stiffened. "My grandmother said you were for real."

Her hurt rushed to me in waves. I glanced toward Jo for help, but none was coming. "I am for real." I fumbled for the right words. "If anyone can define real. I see the emotional imprints people leave behind."

Jo pursed her lips.

Not giving her any time to think, I rushed for another explanation. "Like auras or memories. I've heard them called event projections. Just reflections of past events. Not ghosts."

"Sorry, Lauren." Jo put a hand on her shoulder. "I know how badly you wanted this. And it's a long drive back, and we should get her on the road before—"

"Okay. Okay." Lauren cut her off. Then, without missing a beat, she grabbed both bags out of the car. "We'll let her do it her way and see what happens."

"That's not what I meant," Jo said.

"I know. But she's here now. Give her a chance."

Jo took in a deep breath and threw her a glance full of fondness. She turned to me with a hint of the earlier smile. "Why don't you come in for some coffee or tea before you drive back, and we can go from there?"

"Okay. Thanks." I did want to see the inside of the house. Gran would want a full report on my way home, so I scooted around Jo to follow Lauren up the stairs. The front door itself was gorgeous: a shimmering white, with a black-leaded glass transom above it and windows in the same black lead on either side.

Lauren opened it and stepped inside. "Come on, Edgar. Let's go."

Edgar dropped to his haunches by my car. His ears perked up with his name, but he didn't budge.

"See?" Lauren said to me. "He won't come in. It started almost as soon as they got up here."

"She's right about that. I had to go buy him a doghouse. I hate it. He normally sleeps on my bed." Jo patted me on the shoulder in a friendly way and stepped inside, easy in her fluid movement. "Follow me to the kitchen."

I tried. I really did.

As soon as I attempted to cross the threshold, a jagged force, strong and fierce like nothing I'd ever experienced before, stopped me dead in my tracks. My breath quickened, my body tensed, and the hair on my arms rose straight up like in a horror movie.

"You okay?" Jo asked with a mixture of concern and annoyance.

"I...I don't know." A prickling sensation crept over my skin. I clutched the doorjamb to steady myself.

Jo was there in an instant, wrapping her hand around my forearm. And just like that, the energy or the force or whatever it was, vanished. It didn't recede like an outgoing tide. It was simply gone.

Everything went still, as if house was holding its breath. I felt an odd sense of gratitude for her hand on my arm. Chaos one moment, calm the next.

Lauren jumped to my side, her eyes glowing with excitement. "What is it? Did you see a ghost?" She seemingly hadn't given up on the hope that they were real.

"No." I shook my head, still unsteady, still unsure. Already the reactions of my body were fading. "But I felt something. Something I've never felt before."

"I knew it." Lauren bounced in place.

Jo at her side, pursed her lips, and then said, "What did you feel?"

"Can I sit down?" My legs wobbled, and I needed a second before I could explain something that even I didn't understand.

"Of course." Lauren took my arm and led me into a long hallway.

Up to now, seeing reflections of the past was like a movie, one master shot playing out right in front of me, but nothing physical in any way. If anything, space was always a little dead around the echoes. And there certainly had never been a reciprocal reaction inside me. What on earth had happened at the doorway? And what had caused it? Was it a new incarnation of my gift or something completely new?

I wrapped my arms around myself. I had already lost control with Keera. I wasn't ready for another go around. Lauren sat me at the marble island on a stool and poured water into the electric kettle.

"This didn't start now, you know," she said over her shoulder. "It started before Edgar wouldn't come in. It started with the flowers."

Jo pulled out several boxes from a cabinet. "Coffee or tea, caffeine or herbal?"

"Tea, please." I pointed to a red Twinings box. It was the kind Gran always had in her cupboards.

Lauren continued as if there had been no interruption. "I cut some irises from the garden, and overnight, they died. At first, I thought it was my fault. I'd cut them wrong, or there was something bad in the vase. So I got more, and this time, they wilted almost before my eyes."

"That's a bit of an exaggeration. And flowers die," Jo said.

"Of course they do, but not that quickly. And what about Edgar?"

Jo had the good sense not to answer. Instead, she pulled mugs from another cabinet and put the tea bags inside.

"So tell us what you felt?" Lauren asked instead.

"I don't know. I'm totally out of my depth here." I shrugged, suspecting that she wouldn't rest until I put the moment into words or at least tried. "Something...wild...untamed. Maybe the energy that makes the reflections?" I paused and shook my head. "I've never felt anything like that before."

Lauren nodded rapidly. "Go on."

"Strong emotions. Everyone has them at some point, right? Sometimes, they leave a mark, a kind of imprint that lingers. It's stored energy, and under the right circumstances, it's released as something. A memory? An echo?" I shrugged again. "Don't ask me how or why."

Lauren tilted her head at Jo. "Is that possible?"

What? Jo is the expert now?

She raised her hands as if giving up. "That's basically what the law of conservation of energy says. Energy can't be created or destroyed. It just changes forms."

"So it could transform into one of these reflection thingies?" Lauren's voice was passionate with hope.

"There's no scientific proof, Ren," Jo said quickly but not un-kindly.

"But there's no scientific proof that it can't, right? Something powerful and emotional must have happened here." Lauren stared Jo down until the kettle beeped repeatedly. She busied herself by pouring water into the mugs. "Jo knows all about energy. She's a plasma physicist. Between the two of you, we have experts on both sides."

"I'm not an expert. I have only seen some stuff. Very unscientifically," I added, a little unsettled. I was way out of my depth.

"I'm not an expert either right now. I'm trying to get back to being an expert." Jo gave Lauren a look that wasn't clear to me, but Lauren rolled her eyes.

"Jo is between jobs at the moment. She just got back from France. She's crazy smart and a great scientist. You'll complement each other well. Hazel, let me get this straight. The energy at the door comes before the reflections?"

I shrugged. "Like I said, I've never experienced any energy before. Where the reflections come from or go afterward, I don't know."

"Maybe your powers are growing," Lauren said with certainty. "What do you think?" she asked Jo.

"I've no theories about any of this." Jo shook her head as if literally throwing the thought out of her mind.

Lauren ignored her. "If your theory is true, Hazel, then all we have to do is wait for the reflection to manifest." It wasn't a question; it was a declaration as if everything was decided. She pulled out a milk container from the fridge and shook it gently at me. "Do you take milk?"

"I do."

She poured a dollop into each mug and brought one over to me. *Physics is like magic, but real* wrapped around the mug in big black letters. She held out Jo's so we could both see it. *Think like a proton and stay positive.*

"I wondered where all these cups went." Jo smiled. "For a while, that was the only birthday present I got. Mugs and T-shirts. Which one do you have, Lauren?"

She swiveled hers. *Live in the Moment.*

"As if you need a mug to tell you that." They smiled at each other. "If you're unscientific, what do you do?" Jo asked me.

"Professional animal photographer." I told them about the gallery and the excursions into the wild from the river otters of Solano County to the manatees in Florida whose numbers were dropping again. I left out the celebrities or any of the crazy, money-centric shoots Keera dreamed up. I was careful to paint a picture that I'd like to look at. It occurred to me that I was crafting a reflection of myself and offering it to them. But it didn't matter. As carefully as I curated my own story now, the real truth was out there. I couldn't escape it for long.

During a comfortable lull in the conversation, Lauren leaned over the island to meet my gaze. I liked how immediate she was, maybe too much in the long run, but I lived in a world where people and reflections didn't focus on me. She was a nice change. "Have you ever tried to take pictures of the reflections?"

"In the beginning, of course. Over and over. But it never worked. Occasionally, there was a shimmer in the frame, but that could've been anything. Light refraction, dust in the air, lens flare."

"That's a shame," Lauren said thoughtfully, and then, she was off again. "When will the energy turn into the movie thing you can see?"

I tapped a finger on my mug, the sound barely audible. "I don't know. Your guess is as good as mine."

She answered her own question. "Maybe the house needs to get used to you, and you need to get used to the house."

"Maybe. I've never ever been able to control what I see. Not once."

"That settles it," Lauren said brightly. "Let's give her a tour. She can stay the night. We can get the Blue Room ready, and she and the house can get acquainted."

"Seriously?" Jo gathered the empty mugs and took them to the sink. "Don't you think we've taken this far enough?"

"Not even close." She turned Jo so she was facing her. "I know you think I'm crazy. Something is going on in this house, and we need to listen to it."

Jo rolled her eyes but said nothing.

"I don't know why this is so important to me. But it is. Please?"

They looked at each other, Lauren imploring wordlessly. Jo sighed and dropped her head in defeat.

Lauren grinned. "Thank you."

I watched it all from the stool, an uninvited observer. There was no bitterness in the thought, just quiet resignation. I had always felt safer on the outside. It was way easier. But still, something in my chest twisted, an ache I didn't want to acknowledge. Maybe it was time for a change.

THE LETTERS

The Past: Eliza

April 2, 1925

Dear Joelyn,

What an exciting invitation! Henry and I would be tickled pink to join you and your brother Lewis at the Seals' season opener. Father naturally said no at first. Ladies at baseball games are simply not socially acceptable, but when Mother told him that the invitation came from you, he changed his tune faster than a jazz chord progression. A Hamwell stepping out with a Steward? It knocked his socks off, and he has been throwing your name around without caution. Henry is beside himself with excitement and has been talking about nothing else. He loves Rec Park, as he loves baseball. Did I tell you that? This will be my first game. Henry has been telling me stories that not too long ago, before Prohibition, people got a choice of a ham and cheese sandwich, a whiskey or two beers with their ticket. No wonder everyone loves the game. When I laughed at him, he gave me an earful about Doug McWeeny and how his return to the Seals will put their pitching back on the map. Please don't even get him started Friday night or we'll never hear the end of it. See you then!

Yours,
Elizabeth
The Durham House
Pacific Heights

❖

April 8, 1925

Dear Joelyn,

I simply had to write before bed. Tonight was the bee's knees and then some. The game was amazing! I still don't know how the Seals pulled it out. A 4-4 tie at the end of the game and McWeeny still pitching all the way to the top of the tenth inning. You all said he couldn't throw another pitch after his last strikeout, and then he didn't have to. You were absolutely right to make me stand up for Bower's at bat. I would have kicked myself something awful if I'd missed that homer sailing over the wall. Listen to me with all the baseball words I now know. Henry told me all the way home how lucky we were to see the Seals win 6-4 in extra innings! He also thinks they will win the Pacific Coast League pennant this year. The poor boy couldn't stop talking about how wonderful the night was.

He wasn't the only one on cloud nine. I felt so alive tonight. I don't know whether it was my first taste of champagne, sitting next to you, or the freedom of the night. I know I said this before we parted, but I was touched that you remembered that I had never had champagne and brought a bottle. I felt so scandalous sitting right there in plain view with glasses overflowing. No one even gave us a second look, thank goodness, since there was more whiskey in the stands than water in the entire bay. I should be thankful that San Francisco is said to be the wettest city in America.

Champagne aside, you made the evening pure magic. Father's strict rules and silly regulations were a million miles away. I know it sounds ridiculous, especially since we can count our friendship by only two tennis games and one night out, but anything seems possible when I am in your company. I have never laughed as much with anyone as I have with you. What a wonderful laugh you have. It is like music. You enjoy life more than the rest of us, and it is catching. I want you to know that I feel so lucky to be your friend.

Yours,
Elizabeth

❖

April 9, 1925

Dear Joelyn,
Thank heavens you answered my last letter. I felt like

such a fool when I woke up the next morning with a splitting headache, very little recollection of what I had written, and the letter already on its way to you. Poor Robert was quite put out when I asked him to deliver the letter in the middle of the night. It might have been the champagne talking, and I hope that I did not embarrass you or myself. Did I really write something about your laugh?

Henry is busy this Thursday, and so we must decline your kind invitation to the motion pictures. I have not seen *The Thief of Baghdad*. I hear that Douglas Fairbanks is marvelous. I hope you enjoy it.

Sincerely,
Elizabeth
The Durham House
Pacific Heights

CHAPTER THREE

The Present: Hazel

"In 1847, our grandfather, five greats ago, came to America from Germany," Lauren began. "Claude Stjeward." She pronounced the name with a German accent. "He was nineteen, and he had only one coin in his pocket. Worth seventy-five cents, as the story goes, in today's money. Fifty years later, he had anglicized his name to Steward and had more than enough coins to build this house. He called it Schlosschen Meerblick, Little Castle of the Ocean View." Lauren swung her arm around a grand ballroom complete with crystal chandeliers, inlaid wood floors, and a gleaming grand piano on its own raised stage. "This was his favorite room. Here, he hosted parties that were the talk of San Francisco. A chosen few would be invited out for the weekend, and then, on the last night, he threw a glorious ball with live music and dancing and more food than you could eat in a month."

Jo threw Lauren a pointed look. I kind of wished she'd throw me one too. The kind that was unspoken but full of meaning. The kind that would make my pulse skip, that felt like a secret meant just for me. But we weren't having that kind of conversation.

"Yeah, I know." Lauren dropped her outstretched arm. "There are plenty of stories about how he made his money, and most of them aren't kind to our five-greats grandfather. They called him a sabbath breaker and a hoodlum to his face. Behind his back, it was worse than that."

"A lot worse," Jo seamlessly picked up the story. "He started out as a clerk in a dry goods grocery in New York City. They say he talked himself into a job right off the boat, although he didn't speak a word of English."

Lauren shrugged. "Talking people into things was his superpower."

"You've inherited that a bit. In a good way," Jo said with an indulgent smile.

They were really sweet together, and I knew for certain that both Jo and Lauren were good people. It didn't matter how I ended up at Meerblick, I was lucky to be here.

"Then the Gold Rush happened," Jo said. "Claude was one of the first people who saw an opportunity and sprinted to California almost before Sutter found his first nugget. He wasn't here for the gold, though. He came to fleece the miners. They say he bought pans and picks for twenty cents and sold them for fifteen dollars apiece."

"Can you believe that?" Lauren brushed me on the arm, pulling me into the conversation. "He wouldn't accept anything less. They called him No Credit Claude."

"We still have the ledgers somewhere," Jo said. "There was one month in 1849 when he made one hundred and fifty thousand dollars. In one month. Somebody back then called it: he didn't come for conscience but for coin."

They made a great storytelling team. One jumped in as the other was finishing and drawing us all into the past. Better than a reflection since it was live, brimming with a happy vitality, and I was thrilled to be a part of it.

"People hated him." Lauren shook her head. "And he got much meaner and even richer." She lowered her voice for emphasis.

"Yep. He bought land in Sacramento, kicked out the indigenous people, and rented the land to the miners at astronomical rates. He bought up a lot of San Francisco, and eventually, he ended up here, right on the coast. With this house, he was trying to pretend that he was old money."

"That both he and his fortune were clean."

"That this house wasn't built on the hardships and failures of exploited people."

I felt the weight of their family's past settling in the room between us. I could feel it pressing against them, shaping their present.

"He tried almost too hard to impress." Lauren led us to an ornate fireplace across from the stage, her hand gliding over the marble mantle. She patted the centerpiece, a gilded bronze bust of a bearded man wearing a lion's head. "This is an exact replica, scaled down of course, of the one in the Herculean Salon from the Palace of Versailles. Claude fancied himself a modern-day Hercules. He wore a huge beard his entire life."

"After his death, our family tried to atone," Jo said. "We have always supported numerous charities, but you can never erase the atrocities of the past."

So true. If the reflections had taught me anything, it was that past deeds lived on and on. Echoes lingered, shaping the present in ways we didn't always see. Did she realize how closely our perspectives aligned? I wanted to reach for her, to close the space between us. To let her know that everyone carried the past with them. The reflections I saw and the memories she carried weren't that different. We were already on the same page.

From the ballroom, they guided me through the other public areas of the mansion: grand receiving rooms, separate gentlemen's and ladies' cloakrooms. Finally, we walked into a dining room that could seat a small city. Matching Tiffany & Co. lamps with their original bases greeted us at the door, and the table was laid out with china and silver as if for one of Claude's weekend parties.

"Most of the rooms are closed unless we're hosting charity events," Jo explained as we stood there. "When we come up here, we live in a few private rooms that we had modernized for the twenty-first century, like the kitchen you've already seen. Claude had a codicil in his will that we can't change any of the forward-facing rooms."

"Do you want to see your room?" Lauren asked. Again, without waiting for my answer, she headed out the nearest door. Upstairs, she threw open the door with a flourish and said, "This is the Blue Room, one of my favorites in the whole house."

I could see why. Keera had booked some fancy hotels when we were on jobs—she liked to live in luxury—but this room blew all of them out of the water. The space was serene and calm and drew me in as if it was giving me a comforting hug. The walls were a gorgeous eggshell blue, and huge, multipaned windows looked out into a garden filled with summer color. Linen curtains fluttered gently in the breeze, and the bed was simply an oasis. The matching linen headboard was tacked with antique silver nailheads, and the blankets were equally old-world charm and new-world comfort.

"This is the most beautiful room I've ever seen," I said, already planning to snap a few photos for Gran later.

"Full disclosure," Lauren said with a gleam in her eye, "when Edgar was still coming into the house, he'd come in here and bark at nothing for as long as we'd let him."

"So if you want another room," Jo jumped in, "there are plenty."

"No, this is good." I glanced around and took in the energy of the room. "Sorry, Lauren, I don't feel anything in here."

Her face dropped for an instant. She had no doubt been hoping that I would walk in here and see an instant reflection. I hated to disappoint her. I was actually starting to really like her. But at the same time, I was relieved. I liked being here, caught in their moment, watching their feelings and relationship unfold in real time. I didn't want a reflection to come along and ruin that.

"Great. Then it's settled." Once again, Jo and I were on the same page. "You can get your stuff, and I should pull something out of the freezer for dinner. You hungry?"

"Starving." I hadn't eaten since coffee and a muffin that morning.

Jo, as it turned out, was a fabulous cook. Pulling something out of the freezer translated into fillet steaks with a rich wine and mushroom sauce paired with a delectable salad straight from their garden. I couldn't remember when I'd eaten so well. This trip was beginning to feel less like an obligation and more like an impromptu vacation.

Jo had a lot to do with that. She hadn't wanted me here, but sometime during the tour, maybe even before, she had completely warmed up. At dinner, I was beginning to relax around her as well, something I hadn't done around another woman in a long time. It wasn't just her sultry voice and how she moved like a panther. Somehow, she made the room feel lighter. She had some of five-greats grandfather Claude's charisma as well. Or maybe, for the first time in a long time, I was open to someone else. Jo's laughter and easy nature, now that she was pretty sure I wasn't a ghost hunter, was contagious. But it was more than that. She was drawing me out of myself and the tight space I had been stuck in for too long. Not surprisingly, I liked that. A lot.

"Coffee or something stronger?" She broke into my thoughts as Lauren took the empty dinner plates back to the kitchen. She held my eye for a second longer than seemed necessary. Was she open to me too?

"Something stronger." I wasn't driving, and I wanted to prolong the evening.

"Lauren," she called, "meet us in the salon."

"I should help with the dishes." I got up, but Jo lightly cupped my elbow, pulling me in the opposite direction.

"It's okay. We have a routine. I cook. Lauren washes up. It's worked since we were kids. We can't upset the apple cart."

"You're sure?"

"Ren," Jo called, "Hazel wants to help clean up. Can she?"

"Nope, I totally got it." Lauren's voice rang back cheerfully. "Pour me one of those drinks you brought back from France, please."

Jo gently squeezed my elbow and then let go. "See? She's territorial about her routine. Come on."

She led me to a small room tastefully decorated in soft shades of rose and cream. It was very delicate and feminine, likely designed over a century ago to give women their own space. Low sofas lined each wall, and in the middle of the room was an oval, wooden coffee table with gorgeous bronze roses inlaid in its center.

"This is the Rose Salon," she explained. "But more importantly, it's where Lauren and I hide the good booze." She stepped to a bookshelf between two sofas and pulled at its center shelf. The entire bookcase swung open to reveal a hidden bar with glass shelves and vintage rose wallpaper.

"Originally, they hid the bar because the women in our family drank without anyone knowing. Lauren and I hide it because our male cousins drink all the booze when they come up and don't replace it."

"They don't come in here?" I asked, amused.

"Oh no, this room's way too girly for them. Their loss." She shrugged and pulled out a bottle filled with amber liquid. "Do you know calvados? It's an apple brandy. I brought a couple of my favorite bottles home when I left France. Want to try it?"

"Yes, please." I couldn't distinguish apple brandy from apple juice, but I was enjoying watching Jo move about the cozy room. It had been built to foster intimacy between women. Not the kind that was lurking at the back of my mind, of course, but as a place where women could sit comfortably, have a secret drink, and talk. "How long were you in France?"

Jo poured three generous measures into crystal glassware that tapered elegantly toward the top. "Pretty much my whole life. My mother's French. I went to school and college here, but I spent all my vacations in our farmhouse up in Normandy. When I was there last, I joined a fusion research facility in the south and stayed in the country until the job ended."

I took a tiny sip of the brandy and let it wash over my tongue. "Ooh, it kind of tastes like apple pie."

"Yeah, the same kind of warmth."

"And a little bitterness," I added, savoring the complexity. "But in a good way."

"I always say that drinking something straight is a great way to get to know it." She held up her glass, and the amber liquid caught the light of the room. "As it warms up, the flavors change. It's what this particular distillery is known for. We always make time for a visit when I'm there."

"Are you going back soon? Or are you going to stay here now that your job's over?" I tried to sound casual. Of course, I wasn't asking out of idle curiosity. I wanted to know how long Jo would be in town, but there were a thousand better ways to ask it. Small talk with attractive women had never been my strong suit.

Her face clouded over, and for a moment, I thought she had seen right through me. Her answer, however, suggested something deeper. "I don't know. I'm not sure what's next. I came up here to think. Lauren was kind enough to join me."

"And that's when all the weird shit started happening." Lauren stood at the door of the room with a plate of brownies.

"That was quick," Jo said.

"You clean up as you go along. I've always had the better deal, if you want to renegotiate."

Jo shook her head, took the plate, and handed Lauren the drink. She offered me a brownie, and after a bite, I was surprised by how beautifully it paired with the brandy.

"You know," Lauren sat on her own sofa across the room, "I can't figure out the timing of all this. This house has been in our family for over one hundred years. And it's been in constant use. We even had an uncle who lived here full-time after a divorce, and not one person has ever mentioned anything strange happening. And trust me, our family isn't the kind to suffer in silence."

She laughed at herself, and my lips started to curve into a smile until I glanced at Jo. Her face had clouded over for the second time. Lauren either didn't see or didn't care.

"So why now?" Lauren continued. "I keep asking myself, what's changed?"

She glanced at Jo as if she thought she might take up the conversation like before, but Jo slid her unfinished drink onto a coaster and stood. "I'm going outside to check on Edgar and take him for a walk. If I don't see you before you go to bed, Hazel, good night. We'll get you on the road tomorrow morning." And she left.

So weird. She obviously didn't believe in the reflections, but she had been kind and generous and, half of me thought, even a little flirtatious. And now a switch had been flipped, and the person I'd hoped was becoming my friend, or more, seemed cold and distant. I didn't understand what had changed, but the shift was unmistakable. And for reasons I didn't want to completely embrace, it stung.

"You'll have to excuse her." Lauren pursed her lips while she glanced at the empty door. "She's not herself lately, and Edgar staying outside puts her completely over the edge."

"Is she really that upset about…" I didn't know what to call it. "The strange happenings?" I ended weakly.

"Yes. And no." Lauren hesitated as if not sure she should continue. "It's a bunch of things."

I swirled the drink thoughtfully, taking another sip. Jo had been right; the flavors, like this conversation, were becoming much more complex.

"She didn't come back to the States only because of the job," Lauren said carefully. "Her contract was over, but they offered her another position."

"And she didn't want to stay?"

Lauren shook her head. "No. She had a personal reason for coming home." Another pause while she seemed to weigh whether to continue. "She had a relationship that ended very badly. Jo thought she was the one."

She? And she's single. I tucked those little tidbits away for later. "Oh, I'm so sorry."

"Yeah, me too. It's been a while, but she was emotionally shaken, and that's not like her. She won't tell me what really happened with Camille. It must've been something pretty traumatic. She didn't even want to stay in the country. Normally, she's so calm and so together, and I can't help wondering that maybe…"

"What?"

"Maybe when she brought that emotion up here, she stirred something up? Is that crazy?" She looked at me, her eyes wide with hope and concern.

"I wish I knew," I said honestly. "I'm not trying to put you off or anything. But it's not like there's a reference book where I look up answers."

"I get that now." Lauren rubbed the back of her neck. "Look, don't say anything about Camille. Please. She'd kill me if she knew I brought their relationship up. She won't admit it, and she'll swear to her dying breath that she doesn't believe in whatever's happening up here, but deep inside, she knows she's part of it. That's why she bolted when I brought it up."

"I won't say a word." Poor Jo. It sounded like she had a lot on her plate. Don't get me wrong, I wasn't pitying her. I was relating to her. We all had our struggles. Another connection between us.

"The thing is, I loved seeing her with you today," Lauren's voice softened. "She was more herself with you this evening than she's been with me the whole time we've been here. For a second, she shoved whatever happened with Camille far in the background. I want her to get through this and back to that Jo."

"There's never an easy way through a breakup," I said, more about myself than Jo. But Lauren didn't seem to catch it; she was off and running to the next point.

"Hey, I'm not trying to get rid of you, but maybe if you spend some time in the Blue Room by yourself, you'll see something to help us all out. It could work like that, right?"

"It could, but I don't want to get your hopes up."

"Too late," she said, her smile returning full force. "Let's get you upstairs."

THE LETTERS

The Past: Eliza

April 15, 1925

Dear Joelyn,

I don't know how you charmed my mother into agreeing to let us go to the motion pictures last night. In her way, she is as provincial as Father, even more so since she can trace her family back to common traders in the gold camps. Something in your smile must convince everyone to do exactly what you want. I better be careful. How did you get your servant, our chaperone, to disappear for the film? When I told you Henry was busy, I had no idea that we two would make it an evening. What a treat! I've never seen anything so lavish. Don't try to tell me that the magic carpet wasn't real.

I've been pondering our talk. My upbringing has been very strict, as you know, and I have always been taught that rules are there for a reason. Maybe I'm coming around to your way of thinking that not all rules should be obeyed. Father would have a conniption if he read that sentence. Your take on the picture set me thinking. Fairbanks is a lowly thief in the beginning. If he had played by the rules of society, he would have stayed a thief. Instead, he throws convention to the wind and embarks on all those adventures to prove himself worthy of the princess. He is the only one crazy enough to think a thief could marry a princess, and he sets out to win her while most folks would accept their lot. We never did mention how beautiful she is and how anyone would risk the rules for her, right? It's one thing breaking the rules when you are in some exotic locale with magic surrounding you and quite another when you are stuck in your own stuffy reality.

Do you really think that we should all reach for what we know is right, even though others might not agree? I know you brought up your mother's organizing all the suffragette marches, but not all situations in life are that black and white. I don't know, I need to think about it for a while. Maybe I'm more conventional than I thought. You'll have to help me work on that.

At least the Felix the Cat cartoon came with no deep thoughts attached. I am almost embarrassed to admit that I might believe in magical creatures and fairies. I have been looking for one ever since I got home. If I find one, I hope that I can save his life like Felix did, and the fairy will grant me one wish like in the cartoon. What do you think? Do you want to go to fairyland like Felix? With me? We can have lots of adventures together.

Yours,
Eliza

❖

June 18, 1925

Dear Joelyn,

It feels peculiar to sit down to write you since we've seen each other nearly every day for the last three weeks. But I wanted to let you know that I'll be late tonight. Mother is furious at me. She found the dress! I hid it under the bed, but when Mary was cleaning, she innocently pulled it out, and Mother happened to be in the room. When Mother held it up, I swear, Joelyn, it did look awfully tiny and shiny with the beads swinging everywhere. Mother's face went as red as a tomato, and she could barely form a coherent sentence. She wanted to know where I got a flapper dress, where I was going to wear it, and how could I go out naked all at once. Goodness help me, I started laughing and that, of course, made it worse. She stormed out with the dress, telling me to stew in my own juices. Mary, bless her heart, felt so awful that she brought the dress back an hour later and told me that if she had my figure, she would wear nothing else, morning, noon, or night.

So here's my new scheme. I'll play sick or sorry and skip supper. After they go to bed, I'll slip out as quiet as a mouse. Can you fetch me two hours later than we planned? I know we will miss that singer you wanted to see at the club, but at least we can salvage part of the evening. I can't wait to see you.

  Yours,
  Eliza

❖

June 30, 1925

Dear Joelyn,

  Mother is telling me that we see too much of each other, and even Henry is starting to ask why we don't step out the two of us anymore. It was only when they both mentioned it on the same day that I began to wonder about our friendship. I would rather spend time with you than anyone else in the world. That's not as unnatural as they both are saying, is it?

  I don't think so.

  Yours,
  Eliza

CHAPTER FOUR

The Present: Hazel

Night had crept into the Blue Room, deepening the walls' rich hue and casting moonlit shadows against the floor. Lauren lingered in the doorway, her expression brimming with expectation. I shook my head.

"It can happen," she said over her shoulder on her way out. "There's still time. Good night, Hazel. Sweet dreams, or should I say, energetic dreams." She shut the door on her way out.

Alone, I flipped on a light and dropped onto the bed that was as cushiony as any at a five-star hotel. Such an odd ending to a crazy day. Out of habit, I pulled out my phone. When I turned it on, the number twenty-six in a red circle hung above the text icon at the bottom of the screen.

Jesus, Keera. But a small spark of satisfaction flickered inside me. I'd gotten to her. The texts ranged from pleas to return to stern reminders to be professional to outright demands that I answer her. It was immature, but I ignored them all. Instead, I texted Keera's ex-girlfriend.

Not as crazy as it sounds. Lana was the one sane woman Keera had dated after me. She was an influencer, and as usual, Keera had offered to help build her brand. When that help never materialized, Lana had dumped her. I was the only one who missed her. She'd done her job at the gallery and then some.

Can you stop by the gallery tomorrow and make sure everything's okay? I'm out of town, and Keera's having a meltdown. I'll Venmo you my thanks. If you need to step in, please do, and I'll Venmo more.

Lana's reply was almost instant: *Got it. No problem.*

Relieved, I texted Gran a few beauty shots of the room. *The house is better than you've heard. More tomorrow.*

Finally, I slipped into the ensuite bathroom, larger and more modern than I expected from a house this age. It was dominated by a combination shower-tub, a huge, marble behemoth in the back of the room that was so big, I'd have to take a running leap to get into it in the morning. But tonight, I brushed my teeth, washed my face, and with nothing else to do, climbed into bed.

Sleep was elusive. Both the excitement and the tumult of the day still buzzed through me. So many surprising things had happened, not the least of which was Jo. Thinking about it now, I was a little embarrassed by how completely I'd glommed on to her. How her voice had instantly captivated me on the phone in the morning, how I'd had to stop myself from leaning into her touch when she'd taken my elbow, and how when she'd met my gaze, I'd fallen into those eyes as if they were warm, sparkling pools. Oh my God, had I acted like the infatuated goofball that I obviously was? I wished I could have gone back and seen my actions from the outside and observed myself the way I had so often watched the reflections of others.

However, when I thought about it, why shouldn't I have been interested in Jo? She was single. She dated women. She was easy on the eyes. More than that, she seemed smart, interested, and knowledgeable about a range of things.

Had she felt anything for me?

Stop. I was acting like a middle schooler with my first crush. She had run out of the Rose Salon without a second glance, and despite any fantasy I might entertain now—and I could have dived headlong into that rabbit hole—there wasn't going to be a soft knock on my door in the middle of the night. Most likely, I'd wake up, drive home, and never see her again.

Still, this trip had already given me something. It had pulled me out of the tangle of my life and, for a day, had let me imagine a world beyond Keera. Maybe that was enough.

I closed my eyes, took a few deep breaths, and sleep finally found me.

In my dream, I stood in the Blue Room, though it looked entirely different. The furniture, all antiques when I'd climbed into bed, gleamed with the freshness of just being built. Heavier silk curtains in an art deco pattern covered the windows, and the breeze from the garden had all but disappeared.

Instead, that ragged energy from the front porch buzzed all around me, zipping here and there. In no way alive or conscious, it randomly bounced off the walls like a pinball. Then one jagged bolt hit me square in the chest. Energy coursed from my head to my toes. Images of two women blinked into existence on either side of me, their presence as vivid as if they were truly there. I spun between them. One was dark-haired, the other fair, and both wore silky nightgowns leaving little to the imagination.

I knew I was dreaming and that this wasn't a reflection where I could passively step aside and watch the moment unfold. This moment was playing out around me with me as a participant. The images didn't flow in a neat, linear narrative. They darted and flickered around my mind like a chaotic montage.

The sensation of a kiss brushed my lips.

What the fuck? Was this more than a dream?

The dark-haired woman leaned in, but she wasn't kissing me. She was kissing the fair-haired woman, who responded tentatively. And yet, I felt both kisses. One from in front of me and the other from behind as if I was the conduit through which their passion flowed. I was the connective wiring bringing the images to life. It reminded me of one of those toy plasma balls where the colored energy danced around a glass sphere. I was the central node, and they were the luminous tendrils, their emotions and actions coursing through me to each other.

Our kiss started slow and exploratory, a tentative dance of lips and longing. But as their passion rose, desire leapt up in me as well. I was trapped in someone else's erotic dream, and I couldn't get out.

Not that I really wanted to.

Their bodies closed in. Soft, taut breasts rubbed against my front and back. I floated between their embrace until there was no space separating us. Two hands slid down my back, grabbing me from behind while another set of hands pulled my head back and gently nipped the corner of my mouth. A tongue darted forward, nudging both our lips until they parted. The other woman opened her mouth to the sweet invitation, and so did I, and the three of us were kissing each other.

Three people, two mouths, one unrelenting passion.

Even sound asleep, I knew that this was fucking insane. But I'd spent my entire life thinking the reflections were beyond strange. Who was I to judge? Thanks to Jo, I'd fallen asleep a little wound up, and this dream was the perfect release.

I surrendered.

We were on the bed next, and gentle hands were moving up my legs, leaving trails of heat in their wake. My body buzzed, needy wherever their fingers lingered. And then she was between my legs. One person or two people, I couldn't tell. They pulled me apart and slid one finger inside me. I gasped as they began to stroke in and out, falling into a steady rhythm that quickened every nerve in my body. I was stretched wide until a wonderful melting feeling began to course through me. They drove me toward a blissful release. I arched in response, my body tensing, gathering for that final burst.

But no.

Violently, the dream turned. Without any warning, the passion flashed out with an intensity I'd never experienced. The energy burned from inside, painful and harsh, jabbing me with sharp edges and grabbing me whole when that wasn't enough. It was dragging me down. I'd no idea where, but I'd lose myself if I didn't get out. Pure panic rose in me. I thrashed. I was drowning.

The dark-haired woman manifested between me and the energy. She held out her arms. At first, I thought she was throwing me a lifeline. I reached out for her, desperate to escape.

The energy surged, tearing through the space between us.

"Help me," I either cried out loud or shouted in my mind.

A shiny silver box appeared in one of her outstretched hands. She shook it at me as if that was supposed to be the answer to this nightmare. How the fuck was that going to help?

Before I could act in my dream, the energy lunged out of my body, raced toward her, and forced its way inside. She twisted and turned under its assault, writhing. Her mouth opened wide, maybe screaming but silent. In the dream, like a reflection, there was no sound. The energy grew bigger and brighter, consuming her completely.

In another blinding flash, it came for me.

I woke with a loud, wrenching gasp and sat up so quickly, my whole body spun. I had to get out of there. The energy had followed me from my dream to the waking world. It swirled through the room like a predator, searching for a new target. It wasn't going to be me.

I raced from the room, spun through the hall, and scrambled down the stairs. I made it to the front door and flung it open. The fresh morning air hit me hard like a tonic. I jumped outside and slammed the door on whatever was still in that house.

The Letters

The Past: Eliza

July 8, 1925

Dearest Joelyn,

Father is livid! He saw me going upstairs and literally ran after me and almost wrenched my arm out of my socket to get a better look. He sputtered at me. No actual words, just spit and guttural sounds like an animal while he looked at my hair. I've never seen him in such a state. Not even when Mother told him that the Hamiltons had not invited our family to their Christmas party last year. Now I am sitting in my room waiting for him to collect himself before he comes to talk to me. Oh boy.

We may have gone too far this time. He has always told me that my long blond hair was like his mother's, whom he loved to absolute distraction. By bobbing it, I might have pushed him over the edge. I am, as you know, in the unfortunate position of being an only child. Sometimes, when Father looks at me, he only sees his future grandsons and the heirs of his fortune after he is gone. Although he will never say it plainly, somewhere deep inside, he believes that producing only one measly girl is his great failure. My foremost duty is to give him the sons he could not produce himself. I can almost hear him now. He'll look at me, filled with disappointment, and ask who will want to marry a girl who looks like a common floozy in a speakeasy. Maybe he'll add, do I ever think about anyone but myself when I commit these unnatural and scandalous acts?

Joelyn, whatever happens, it was worth it. Even though I am scared about what might come next, I absolutely love sitting here tossing my head around, feeling my hair hit the bottom of my neck. I never realized how heavy all those knots and buns were and how much of my life I had wasted by twisting every strand up to look as dignified as my grandmother. The more I think about it, when I watched all those locks fall to the floor this afternoon, I felt released. Does it sound so outlandish to say that when I lost my hair, I found myself? I am not my parents' hopes and dreams. I have to live my life for myself.

So come what may, I'll be fine as long as I have you by my side.

With Love,

E

❖

July 20, 1925

Dear Joelyn,

They won't speak to me. They barely let me out of my room. Mary brings me supper on a tray like I am an invalid. Who is being childish now? I am too blue to write. Will this ever end?

Yours,

Eliza

❖

July 22, 1925

Dear Joelyn,

You are absolutely brilliant! The silent treatment from both my parents was unbearable, and then you swoop in to find a way forward.

When your mother rang up and asked my parents to come to a small dinner at their house honoring Mayor Sonny Jim and his good works for the city, my parents were beside themselves with joy. Practically walking on air. My father knows that small means exclusive and can't wait to corner "my friend, the mayor of our fine city," as he now calls him and advance his own profitable agenda for his grocery business. Mother, she is in seventh heaven. An invitation from your family is all she has ever wanted. She is looking at the Social Register right now to see where our name will appear with its next printing.

The best part is that they have forgotten all about me. They even let Henry into the parlor for the first time in almost two weeks. He comes with exciting news. His jazz band has been granted a tour of the northwest. He leaves for Seattle tomorrow, and they will perform up there for a few months before he returns to San Francisco, hopefully with a real following and a name for himself. He says he is committed to making it big, and that there is no real future for him here. I am so excited for him. I'll miss him, of course, but we all have to follow our path wherever that might lead.

What shall we do first now that I am released from prison? Send an automobile around for me tonight after my parents leave for your house. I can't wait to see you.

Yours,
E

❖

July 30, 1925

Everything is all set. My parents finally agreed to let me go to your beach house with your family. They had their reservations, naturally. It's all very well and good when they can use your family and their standing for their own schemes, but in the end, they are too conservative for your family. Mother doesn't even vote now that she can, and yours marched for it. I'll be ready for your parents' automobile at nine in the morning, and don't fret about the arrangements. I don't care if some of the bedrooms are being renovated. It will be great fun to share a room. We can talk and laugh all night.

Yours,
E

❖

August 5, 1925

Stop trying to telephone. Stop trying to contact me by post. I do not ever want to hear from you or think about what happened at the beach house ever again.

CHAPTER FIVE

The Present: Hazel

Outside the house, the sun rose over the cypress trees to the east. Its glow was pale and feeble, but at least it wasn't the menacing darkness from upstairs. Gasping, I was still in the clutches of the dream. My mind reeled, and I couldn't find my center.

I sank to my knees and pulled myself into a sitting position against the wall of the house, my body and mind completely drained. In my exhaustion, I still fought the battle upstairs.

Something wet and warm touched my cheek. I flinched, shrinking back against the house.

What the fuck? The energy is out here too?

But it whined, a soft plaintive sound, and crawled into my lap, repeatedly licking my cheek and nose. *Oh my God. It's Edgar.*

As much as I wasn't ready for him, he saved me. His insistence banished the energy that lingered in my mind and brought me back to myself. I found my center and opened my eyes to his puppy dog smile.

Except for my childhood dog, Atticus, I'd never loved a dog so much. I buried my face in his fur, wrapping my arms around him. He rested his chin on my shoulder. Gradually, the edges of my panic began to dull. A calmness began to move through me, and while I'd not forgotten what happened, the feelings, the emotions started to fade.

I didn't know how long we sat there. It could've been two minutes or two hours before I started to feel more like myself. Long enough for the morning chill to creep into my bones. I'd run out of the house in shorts and a T-shirt, woefully unprepared for the weather. I thought about going to my car, but my keys were inside. Going back up there wasn't an option.

I heard Jo's voice before I saw her. That rich, beautiful voice reached me like a lifeline. "He likes you."

My eyes popped open. She stood on the front step in jogging gear and an expression so neutral, it couldn't have been natural.

Heat rushed into my cheeks, and I would've bet hard money my face was glowing red. This wasn't the way I wanted to meet Jo this morning. I tried to get up, and Edgar, maybe sensing that I still needed him, hunkered down. We rolled around on the porch and eventually ended up where we'd started.

Jo chuckled. "Yep, he really likes you."

"He's a wonderful dog." And to prove my point, he stretched out in my lap. "You must be wondering why I'm out here at the crack of dawn and all."

"I'll admit, the question did cross my mind." She left it hanging as a faint smile played on her lips, but she quickly rescued me. "I get up early now to make sure Edgar is okay. I don't understand why he's not coming into the house anymore."

I did. But telling her would only make me sound crazier than she probably already thought I was.

"I guess today I could've slept in," she said, her smile widening a little. "If I'd known you'd be out here."

Shoving my embarrassment aside, I met her gaze. Her eyes were warm with concern, looking at me as if I were a lost child.

"Normally, he's a lot shier with people he's just met."

"Well, we've bonded this morning." I ran a hand through my hair, trying to smooth my curls. I couldn't even imagine how I looked.

"I can see that." Her laugh was soft and teasing. "Do you want to come back inside? There's coffee already brewed. It's organic. We get it from a guy who roasts it himself."

I sighed. "I'm not sure I can."

Her gaze sharpened, but she didn't push. "Okay. I'll get two cups and come back outside."

Her calmness lingered after she left. It washed over me and soothed my jagged nerves. What would it be like to have that kind of steadiness in my life? I was tired of always being on edge.

Edgar slid from my lap with a look back, as if to make sure I was okay. He wandered over to the grass, sniffing the ground as he went. His warmth gone, the cold morning air nipped at my bare arms and legs.

When Jo returned, she carried two cups and, thankfully, a fuzzy throw. She handed me the blanket first and held out both cups. One was brown with cream and the other a glossy black. "I don't know how you take it."

"Cream." I reached out, then hesitated. "But either will be great."

"Perfect. I like it black. Sugar?" She magically produced a few packets from her jacket pocket.

"No, thanks." I wrapped my hands gratefully around the steaming cup. Between it, the blanket, and Jo's kindness, I began to feel more like myself.

She dropped to my side on the porch in a poised, effortless move. We sat in silence for a moment, our backs to the wall. Finally, knocking her shoulder against mine, she said, "Look, I need to apologize for last night. Lauren knows exactly how to get under my skin, and I couldn't hear any more of her theories about how the house is reacting to my emotions."

So Jo knew that Lauren thought the house was tied to her.

"But you look a little freaked out, and while I may not believe what you're going to tell me, I'd like to hear it. I promise to listen with an open mind."

I nodded and swallowed. Why not? They could do whatever they wanted with the knowledge. This was their story, not mine, after all. "Can we get Lauren out here? I don't know if I can tell it more than once."

"Good idea." Leaving her coffee on the porch, she jumped up even more gracefully. "I'll go get her," she said and disappeared for the second time back into the house.

Lauren must have been asleep because when she stumbled through the front door, she was in a robe and her pajamas, rubbing her eyes. She plopped down beside me, nearly trembling with expectation.

Jo reappeared with a third cup and silently handed Lauren it and two packs of sugar. They sat still and expectant, waiting for me to begin.

I started at the very beginning: seeing my first reflection at age six in my bedroom. I told them about Gran and how she trained me as if I was in some wizard school. "Neither of us knew what we were doing. We still don't."

Lauren's leg bounced in little jerks as she itched for me to get to the good part. Jo, on the other hand, listened with the attentiveness she had promised. Her shoulders dropped, and she leaned back on both arms when the story didn't veer off into nutty ghost lady territory. The corners of her lips ticked upward when I told them about Atticus and how my camera had captured the energy there. I was trying to explain how it was more than the reflections.

"You see, it's all around us," I said, gesturing with my free hand. "Everywhere. All the time."

"Yes. We get it." Lauren leaned in, her impatience bubbling over. "What you're calling energy exists. But how does any of this connect to last night?"

Jo put a gentle hand on Lauren's shoulder to prevent her from creeping forward even more. "She'll get to it."

"Honestly, last night brings up more questions than it answers," I mused.

"Oh, perfect. I love a puzzle." Lauren's smile returned, her optimism rebounding as she sat back. "Tell us everything."

I opened my mouth to do that, but the words stuck in my throat. How could I explain a three-way kiss or the ménage à trois on the bed? I didn't want to come off as twisted or perverted. I cared too much about what they thought. So I chickened out and eventually described the dark-haired woman who seemed to be at the center of it all.

"I knew we had a ghost," Lauren said when I finished. "But who? Clarissa maybe? She had dark hair, and she built the house as much as Claude did. It would make sense that she'd still be here."

"Can we stop calling them ghosts? Hazel clearly said it was a dream. And for the record, every woman in our family has dark hair."

But Lauren was already off and running. "Clarissa was Claude's daughter," she explained to me before swiveling back to Jo. "Maybe her spirit, or energy, if you prefer, is upset for you, Jo. And is trying to help? Trying to send you a message?"

Jo turned to me. "That's not the way the reflections work. Is it?"

I shook my head. "They're never interactive, and this, as I said, wasn't a reflection."

"What's the difference?" Lauren's brow furrowed.

"Usually, I'm an observer, never a participant." My cheeks burned as the kiss from both sides replayed briefly in my mind.

"And last night was different?" Lauren's eyes narrowed. She knew I was holding something back.

"Yes. Something was…in my head. Not a person or spirit," I quickly added for Lauren's benefit. "But the energy…it came at me like a force. It latched on and wouldn't let go. I had to get out. Honestly, I don't know what would've happened if I'd stayed."

"Told you," Lauren said softly.

"All right. I'll give you that," Jo said, her voice calm. "But what do we do now?"

Both Lauren and Jo looked at me expectantly. Even Edgar, trotting along the porch toward us, stopped and fixed me with his gaze.

"I've no idea." I shrugged. "For me, this is where the story ends. If someone could grab my stuff from upstairs. I can get on the road and out of your hair." None of my little fantasies about Jo would come true if I left, but staying here was impossible.

Lauren's eyes widened in disbelief. "Are you kidding? You're not going anywhere. Except, I hope, back upstairs."

Panic rising, I stood up. "I don't think I can."

Lauren jumped up too. "Give it a try. We'll be with you. Jo is the strongest person I know. She'd never let anything happen to you. We've got to get to the bottom of this." She gently grabbed my arm.

"Lauren." Jo rose protectively. "She doesn't want to. You can't make her—"

"Oh my God!" Lauren shrieked and pointed at the front door.

I froze refusing to look. *God, no. Not again.* I imagined the energy snaking out of the door in long tentacles, searching for me. The thought scared me so much, I recoiled on instinct, stumbling straight into Jo's arms. More accurately, she caught me and pulled me into her. I buried my head in her shoulder. I didn't want to see if anything was coming for me.

"Hazel. It's okay." She squeezed me, then turned me toward the door. "Look."

Her voice was low and soothing. Lauren was right. She'd never let anything bad happen to me. I swung to the door. Unbelievably, Edgar's shaggy brown head peered at us from inside the entry hall.

"He's inside," Lauren whispered.

"Oh, Edgar," Jo said, her voice full of love and relief.

Edgar had no idea what he had done, but tail wagging, he bounced out to lick Jo's hand and nonchalantly headed back inside as if there had never been a reason not to.

"He doesn't feel it anymore." Lauren darted past us to throw the door wide open. She waved her arm inside the foyer dramatically. "Nope. Nothing. You must have changed it, Hazel. Now you can go back in. We all can." To prove her point, she triumphantly jumped into the house.

I wasn't so sure. Jo gave my shoulder another squeeze before following Lauren. She sank to the tile floor of the entryway and gathered Edgar in her arms. "Good boy. You're such a good boy."

He snuggled into her without a care in the world. The truth was clear: Edgar didn't feel the energy anymore. Like a canary in a coal mine, he was singing.

I bit my lip and rolled my head weighing my options. Maybe the energy was gone. Or changed. But if Edgar felt safe…

Besides, all my stuff was upstairs, and thinking about it now, I had no idea what shape the room was in. I wanted to see it before Jo did. I cared a lot about what she thought of me. Probably too much.

Dang it. I was going back in.

I pulled the blanket tighter around me like a shield and slowly walked to the door. Inside, Jo, Lauren, and Edgar waited for me eagerly. Lauren held out her arms as if I was a child taking her first steps.

I pressed my palm over the threshold as a test. Edgar was right. Nothing really. Maybe a slight buzzing, but I could handle it.

"You okay?" Lauren wanted to know.

I nodded.

"Good. Come on. Let's go upstairs," she said, already halfway there.

I hesitated.

"Only if you want to," Jo reassured me. She placed one foot on the bottom stair as a gentle invitation. No pressure emanated from her, just the overwhelming feeling that she'd support me whatever I decided.

Was it crazy to go back to the Blue Room? Because the foyer was clear didn't mean the energy wasn't simmering upstairs, waiting to strike. As if answering my question, Edgar trotted up.

I bit my lip and shook my head. What the hell. "I'm not sure I do, but I'll give it a try."

Jo smiled, her warmth reaching me in a way that steadied my nerves. "I'm not sure I want to, either."

I gave a half laugh. "Then for sure, let's both go."

THE LETTERS

The Past: Eliza

Sept 8, 1925

Dear Joelyn,

I find it a little unnerving to sit at my desk to write to you. In the past few weeks, I have written numerous letters only to tear them up. I can barely make sense of my thoughts, let alone put them on paper. All I know is that, try as I might, I cannot put what happened at Meerblick out of my mind. I must struggle to make sense of it. Forgive me if I return to it here to do so.

It all started with the automobile ride up to the house. It was positively intoxicating to be with adults who were not correcting my every move. When your mother asked me what I thought about the recent Scopes Trial and evolution in general, I realized for the first time that neither of my parents had ever asked me about my thoughts or ideas. I don't think I was allowed to have them. That is, of course, an exaggeration, but I am sure you catch my meaning. The freedom that surrounds your family enfolded me and pulled me in. Mind you, I am not trying to excuse what happened later, only trying to understand how it came to be.

The first day on the beach was almost magical. I know you were there, but the trip started out so wonderful. A rare sunny day, racing into the ice-cold waves, building that swell sandcastle with your little sister Helen, your mother reading out loud to us from *Their Eyes Were Watching God* by that Harlem writer. I forget her name. Then that gorgeous picnic full of champagne, Lewis snapping pictures of it all with his new camera. It was like heaven, and later at dinner, I remember thinking I had never been so happy. Your family was buzzing, discussing whether the United States should have quotas for immigrants, and Lewis tried to recreate one of Harry Houdini's escapes with those ridiculous chains he brought up from the city. I can't even begin to tell you how different it was from evenings at my parents' house.

That night, when we got into bed, I was so tired from the excitement of the day that when I tried to stay up to talk to you, I couldn't. I don't even remember falling asleep. When I woke up to find us in each other's arms, I admit that at first, I was startled. Then I realized how comfortable it felt, and I lay there with you. The bed was warm, I was still a little sleepy, and we fit together so perfectly. If it had ended there, I would have never given it a second thought. We were best friends, after all. Then you woke up and looked at me with those dark shining eyes and laughed. Maybe it was that laugh. I've always said you have the nicest laugh I've ever heard, soft and almost conspiratorial. Or maybe it was your face looking at me so expectantly. Maybe it was the magic, a kind of energy that surrounded us. I don't know. Believe me, I have gone over the next moment in my mind at least a thousand times. Joelyn, I don't know why I kissed you. It would have been easier to understand if it was a kiss that one sister gives another, and I have certainly tried to recast it as such in these weeks afterward. If I am honest with myself, it wasn't. I found your lips, and I lingered there, tasting you and feeling what seemed like sparks washing over me until I pulled away.

I couldn't read your reaction. I thought it was a mixture of amusement and something much deeper. I know now that it was longing, but at that time, I was still innocent. My face went hot with embarrassment, and I am sorry that I wouldn't talk to you for the rest of the day. I alternated wildly from thinking I had to find an excuse to go home to feeling like I had to get back into your arms. Every time I met your eyes that day, I would experience feelings that Henry never gave me. Then embarrassment took over again, and I tried not to look at you. I was so tormented by these new emotions and feelings. I didn't even think about what could happen or how I felt about it all. Believe me, I spent the whole day rehearsing how I would tell you that I needed to sleep on the couch downstairs or even how someone needed to drive me home. When I tried to open my mouth to say it, I couldn't. I wanted to, I did, but I also wanted to see what came next. I have never been as torn up inside as I was that day.

Dinner that second night was excruciating. The salmon was divine, the conversation as lively as the night before, but I couldn't focus on a blessed thing. My mind was racing to the time when we would go to bed, both dreading it and wanting nothing else in the world. Then the moment was there. We were both standing by the bed in our nightdresses. I remember looking at you only to notice for the first time how sheer yours was. I could see clear as day the outline of your body underneath it, the soft curve of your bosom, the hardness of your stomach, and the mysterious shadows even lower. My breath went ragged.

I've tried to convince myself that I was led astray, that you pulled me down a path that I did not wish to descend. Now, after a month of thinking about virtually nothing else, I must admit that if a magic carpet had plucked me out of that room, I would have done anything to get back to you.

The next morning brought the harsh light of reality to what we had done. Joelyn, as much as I was born anew that night, I know what happened was unnatural and absolutely wrong. I couldn't even look at you since every glance brought fresh waves of shame and horror. I am sorry if my silence hurt you. I wish we could have talked about it then and there and agreed to forget what had happened. Maybe if we could have closed the page once and for all, I could live with it now.

Please thank your family for making the special arrangements to drive me home early. I am sure that I did not thank them at the time. My parents were upset to see me so distressed, and I must have spent a week in bed pretending to be ill. I certainly was in my mind. I spent ages trying to reconcile the pleasure with these deviant actions. Joelyn, I can't. Everything I have ever learned tells me what we did was wrong. I have tried to reconcile myself with it, but I cannot. We can never see each other again.

Elizabeth

CHAPTER SIX

The Present: Hazel

When we got to the Blue Room, Lauren and Edgar were already inside. Lauren stood in the center of the room with her eyes closed and her arms stretched out in a new age pose. She hummed softly while sweeping the air toward her in big scooping motions. I guessed she never did anything halfway. As someone often pushed to the sidelines, I wondered what it would be like to have that kind of confidence.

Edgar looked at her and cocked his head as if trying to make sense of it all. No. Wait a second. He wasn't looking at her.

Holy shit! Right behind Lauren was a reflection.

My breath caught in my throat. I recognized her instantly. The dark-haired woman from my dream. She shimmered faintly at the edges like a hologram, but her features were sharp and clear in this iteration. She was young, about my age and startlingly pretty, with clear skin and an athletic body. She was dressed in the sheer white nightgown that had fluttered sensuously about me last night. She walked with purpose across the room, clutching the shiny silver thing from my dream. Then it had seemed like a weapon. Now it was a box for keepsakes.

She stepped away from Lauren, who was completely oblivious to the one thing she desperately wanted to see. I had a vague sense that Lauren was explaining her actions, and Jo was laughing and teasing her in response. But their reality faded into the background. I stepped around Lauren to get a better look because suddenly, I was standing at the back wall.

The woman stared at the box in her hand for a long moment, her face blotched and pinched as if she had been crying. She turned her head slightly to the door, hearing a sound I couldn't. With a sense of urgency, she pressed the box up against the wall.

Her hand, the box and everything, vanished as if the wall had gobbled them up. She looked intently into the space, and her handless arms did something I couldn't see. Her whole body heaved in a deep, soundless sigh, and she pulled her arm out of the wall. She had left the box inside.

Her movements slowed. She turned to the bathroom door, her shoulders heavy with defeat, and shuffled across the room. I stepped aside to let her pass. Of course, the woman wasn't aware of me. She was caught in her own time, doing exactly what she had done all those years ago. This was an echo. A reflection. I followed her to the bathroom door, and as she crossed the threshold, she shimmered into nothingness.

Lauren grabbed my arm from behind and spun me around. "You saw something. What?" Her face was an odd mixture of excitement and envy.

Jo was right there, concern welling in her eyes. "Give her a minute, Ren. You okay?" She put her hand on my arm.

I nodded. "Yeah." And I was. For the first time since I'd pulled my car into their driveway, I meant it. The reflection had been off-putting and pulled me out of my present but was no different than any other reflection from the last twenty-six years. It was almost comforting that we were back to feelings that I knew well.

"Oh my God. What did you see?" Lauren almost burst at the seams.

I took a deep breath and laid out the story as meticulously as I could. Even so, there wasn't enough detail for Lauren. She dragged me into the center of the room so I could act out the reflection in the role of the dark-haired woman from beginning to end.

When we got to the part where the box disappeared into the wall, Lauren frowned in confusion. "She shoved the box inside the wall? How could her arms disappear?"

"I don't know how, but I might know why." I paused, trying to frame it in a way that made sense. "I've seen it before. Plenty of times. The reflection is decades old, maybe more. The room must've had a different configuration when the memory was recorded. A wall has been added or changed since then. The woman is going through the motions from her time, but the location is from ours. I only see the people. Does that make any sense?"

Jo gave me a small nod, and Lauren cocked her head thinking.

"Oh my God, Jo, remember when we were in York, England, and we went on that ghost tour?"

"Yes. Not my idea."

"You said you liked it. But anyway, the guide, she was super cool, told us a story about the Roman legion marching in a cellar of some famous house. She said the soldiers were chopped off at the knees, remember? The rest of their legs and feet vanished into the stone floor. She explained that the Roman road was buried like a foot and a half lower than the modern floor. So the legion was marching on their road from their own time." Her eyes flashed with sudden understanding. "That's how the reflection works too, right?"

"Probably." I hadn't heard that particular story, and I'd heard a lot. But it made perfect sense to me. That sounded a lot like a reflection.

"Man, I wish I could see what you can." Lauren glanced around the room, clearly willing a reflection to pop up.

"Me too. You would eat these visions up." If I could've waved a magic wand and transferred my gift to her, I would've. Lauren was wired for it. She was excitable and over-the-top, sure, but she had a natural vibrancy that could easily carry the weight. She'd embrace the chaos in a way I never could. Unfortunately, life didn't come with an easy transfer button.

Lauren, however, was already chasing a new thought. She pointed at the wall. "Where exactly did she put the box?"

"About here." I crossed to the wall and dropped a finger on the wall where the woman's arm had vanished.

Lauren bounded over to the desk and plucked a pen off its wooden surface.

"Here?" She poised the pen about an inch off the wall.

When I nodded, she drew a big X as if it were a treasure map.

"What are you doing?" A horrified Jo joined us.

"Marking the spot," she said simply. "We're going after that box." Jo groaned softly. "Oh shit, here we go again."

THE LETTERS

The Past: Eliza

November 20, 1925

The irony of seeing you two days ago has not escaped me. After weeks and weeks of trying to avoid you at the Athletic Club and our usual haunts, I run into you at Crystal Palace of all places. Father routinely likes to look at the grocery competition, and he goes down to that open market to study the patterns of how people move from stall to stall. He is remarkably good at recognizing people's behavior as long as they are not related to him. I was there because Father insisted that I get out of the house, and I agreed because I fancy the strawberry ice cream there. Joelyn, when I spotted you, I nearly turned tail and ran. I would have too, if I had not been at the end of the row and, truthfully, the sudden relief of seeing you had not hit me like a ton of bricks.

I have to admit that feeling was an utter surprise. I have tried my level best these last two months to forget you. I thought I was making headway too. It's been easier since Mother and Father have stopped asking why we do not see each other anymore. I made up some baloney about you being wrapped up in some museum project. Mother doesn't give a hoot anyway since she is busy doing charity work with Mrs. Littney. She milked that one dinner at your parents' house for all that it was worth and more. Since she hasn't been happier, why would she notice that I've never been more miserable?

I had convinced myself that I was on the mend. There were a few moments in the day when I could think about what to have for supper or what to wear the next day. And I would think, this is what it feels like to be customary again. But it was a lie, and I was fooling myself. Seeing you there laughing with your gorgeous dark hair swinging about your face told me plain as day that I will never forget you.

Whatever happened between us got under my skin. What are we to do?

Eliza

❖

November 22, 1925

Yes. I love you too.

❖

Nov 25, 1925

Dearest Joelyn,

Last night was like coming home after an endless winter. I barely remember the Chaplin film, although I do recollect something funny about someone eating a shoe. Just being able to sit next to you for all that time, caressing your hand, and dreaming about being in your arms. You are right that we have to find a way to be alone together.

E

CHAPTER SEVEN

The Present: Hazel

I hopped around the Blue Room, one foot in my jeans leg and one hand on my phone reading texts. I was failing at both tasks. Ten minutes before, Lauren had rushed from my room, dragging Jo and Edgar with her.

"I've an idea," she had said. "Meet us downstairs."

I wanted a shower, but not even a day into this adventure, I already recognized Lauren's "don't mess with me" tone. As I wondered how nice it would be to have everyone swept along by my enthusiasm, my phone blew up.

Text after text hit the screen, dinging louder with each one. Keera had started probably the second she woke up:

Are you getting these?

I need an ETA on when you'll be back.

The NY deal is dying.

They R talking to another fucking photographer.

In my mind's eye, I could see her sprawled on her cloudlike bed, bolstered by a thousand pillows, tapping away on her phone. Was Cherry beside her? Probably. She liked to be *serviced* in moments of stress.

Why aren't you answering me?

Then a bunch of emojis popped up that made no sense. She sent the barfing one with the green vomit five separate times in a row. Her attack ended with one last text.

Stop ghosting me.

I laughed out loud at that one; of course, she hadn't meant the word literally or ironically. I took it as advice and not the thinly veiled threat she meant. Without writing one text, I threw the phone on the bed and finally slid into my jeans. My getaway bag held jeans and a T-shirt, but the pants were cut well for my figure, and the T-shirt was a graphic of one of my dolphin photographs. Was it too self-promotional? Keera had called it good advertising and had forced a dozen on me. They had lived in my car trunk until one had found its way into the overnight pack.

No one was in the kitchen when I came down after making the bed and straightening up the room.

"Hazel? We're in here," Lauren called from one of the many random rooms.

Jo's voice followed with clearer instructions. "Take a right from the back of the kitchen. Follow the hallway to the end. We're on the left."

Count on Jo to guide me there. To make sure, she was in the hall to meet me. She hadn't changed out of her jogging gear, and without the morning trauma clouding my mind, I could take her in properly. Leggings and a matching blue jacket clung to her body like a second skin and highlighted long lean muscles and curves.

"Nice shirt," she said, eyeing my chest. "One of yours?"

Blushing a little, I nodded, and she stepped closer to examine the photograph more closely, staring right at my breasts. "I like it a lot."

Now I blushed a lot. "I've an extra one in my car if you want," I said, immediately regretting it. She was probably being polite, and even to my ears, I sounded overeager.

She put me out of my misery. "Cool. That would be great."

Like the night before, she took my elbow. The touch, so feather-light it was almost not there at all, sent shivers up my arm. My heart fluttered as she led me into the room on the left. "Brace yourself. Lauren's been busy."

The study, another stunning space, was paneled in dark wood, with French doors that opened onto the lush garden. And it looked like a tornado had swept through it. Cabinets stood open, folders were strewn on almost every surface, and the coffee table in the center of the room held dozens of loose photographs. How Lauren had done so much damage in so little time was truly a miracle.

"I brought emotional support drinks," Jo said. Glasses of orange juice, lattes, and even a bright green smoothie sat on a silver tray. "Help yourself."

I grabbed an orange juice.

Jo gave Lauren a green drink. "Okay, so what'd you find? You look like a cat who ate the canary."

"Sit. Let me show you." She directed us to thick pillows surrounding the coffee table. Once we were both cross-legged on the floor, she pulled three photos front and center. "Clarissa Steward."

The photos showed the same woman at different stages of her life. In one, she wore a shiny flapper dress, her hair styled in a short, finger-waved cut, and with dark kohl ringing her eyes. In another, later than the 1920s, her hair flowed longer and softer over an elegant gown that could only be described as couture, maybe even an original Dior. In a third photo, she was about sixty and looked so natural, like the girl next door, with pearls and a matching dress and coat. Not exactly pretty, she was bold and met the viewer's eye as if challenging them to look away. Together, the three images told the visual history of the many faces of Clarissa. None was the face of the woman upstairs.

"Was this who you saw?" Lauren asked.

I hated to burst her bubble. "No. I'm sorry. It wasn't Clarissa."

Her shoulders dropped. "Damn. I was so sure."

"Sorry." Jo touched Lauren's arm, then dropped to Edgar's curly head, which was glued to her side. Jo seemed like a natural at connecting through touch. My elbow, Lauren's arm, Edgar's head. She might have a calm exterior, but she was kind and sensitive and clearly wanted to be connected to people and animals. Sitting there, sipping what turned out to be freshly squeezed OJ, I wondered if I wanted to be truly connected to her. I'd experienced sparks the day before, but was it something more?

"Mmm," Lauren said. "It could be Helen. Her daughter." She dug into the pile on the coffee table and pulled out another photograph of a woman with the Steward features. Dark hair and eyes, and the smile was brighter and more inviting than Clarissa's.

I shook my head, and Lauren leaned back on her heels, frowning with frustration. "The only woman left is my mom, Sarah, but she wasn't even born in the timeframe of the reflection, if our guess is right." She produced a photograph of a woman sitting on the beach wearing a Blondie concert T-shirt and grinning Lauren's grin at the camera.

"It's not her."

"Yeah, I didn't think so. Jo, any ideas?"

"No, my Steward relatives are all male," she said to me. "We have a boatload of boy cousins, but Lauren and I are the only females in our generation."

Lauren gasped and dramatically clasped a hand over her mouth. "Wait! Clarissa had three kids. There was another daughter."

"What?" This seemed like news to Jo.

"Yes, Grandpa found her when he was cataloging everything that summer. I remember him telling me about it."

Jo pressed her lips tight. "He never told me. *You* never told me."

"You and your family had moved to France at that point, and I must have forgotten when you came home." She rolled her head as if trying to bring the memory back. "Grandpa said there were pictures of her, and then there weren't. She was erased from the family record. Grandpa thought there was a family scandal, but he didn't know what."

"That sounds like a real mystery," Jo said.

Lauren nodded. "Her name was Joelyn, like you."

"Joelyn. That's pretty," I said before I'd thought about it.

"It's a family name, but I never knew where it came from. No one ever calls me that."

"You're Jo through and through." Lauren was at a cabinet over on the far wall, rummaging around in the filing system. "Ta-da." She flung both hands in the air in victory.

Both Edgar and I started at her cry. He wasn't totally over his ordeal. Neither was I, apparently.

Lauren slid a photograph onto the coffee table. "A family portrait in 1925."

We all hovered over the picture, our heads nearly touching. Jo was so close, I could smell her shampoo. Fresh and sultry scents of jasmine and sandalwood. I had a hard time focusing on the people on the coffee table until Lauren's tapping on the picture brought me back.

"What about her?" she asked, pointing to a woman in an old-fashioned bathing costume that looked remarkably like a modern tank top and bicycle shorts.

A chill ran through me. The dark-haired woman from upstairs stared out of the past right at me. She stood next to Clarissa, her arm looped casually around her shoulders. Clarissa with her imperious stance should've been the focal point, but her daughter, because that was who she had to be, even in this ancient gelatin print, commanded the frame. A smaller blonde to her left leaned into her as if she wanted to bask in her glow as well. No wonder. A century away, I could almost feel the heat. Who was this woman? Odd that her life force, for want of a better word, could be recorded in a photograph and not come through at all in the reflection upstairs. I'd have to tell Gran and—

Wait a second...

What the fuck?

The second woman. Was she the blonde? Were both women from my dream here in this photograph?

Lauren pulled me back. "Hazel?"

"That's her." I pointed to Joelyn to put Lauren out of her misery.

"We found her." Lauren breathed a sigh of relief.

"Sure, and that's Clarissa. Helen. Lewis, our great, great, great grandfather." Jo pointed to each one as she said their names. "But who's that?" Her finger lingered over the pale blonde who looked so desperately out of place next to the dark-haired giants.

"I don't know. Maybe a.friend? A cousin? Is there anything on the back?"

Jo flipped the picture over and read the neat script out loud, "Beach, summer, 1925. Mother, Helen, Lewis, Eliza, and Me. Wonderful Day."

Eliza. Now I had a name for the woman from last night. Her passion had started tentative, but man, had it exploded. Hard to believe looking at the timid creature in the photograph.

Eliza and Joelyn. What on earth could their story be?

"Does she look like the reflection you saw upstairs? I mean, we have the person, but do we have the time?" Lauren whirled the photo around to take a better look.

I studied the photograph again. "Almost exactly. The reflection must have been recorded in the summer of 1925."

"Excellent. Mystery solved. Are we good?" Jo sat back against the sofa.

"As if. Like I said, we're just getting started. Look." She glanced around the room as if she had meant it literally. "I'm going upstairs to shower and change. Did you get a chance?"

I shook my head.

"Go," Jo said. "I'll make breakfast, and we can all meet in the kitchen in let's say, a half hour?"

"Perfect. Thanks, Jo." Lauren scooted out.

"Are you sure that's okay?" I didn't want her to think that I expected all this hospitality and luxury treatment.

"Of course. Go."

In the hallway, Lauren was waiting for me. "Come get me immediately if you see anything else."

I nodded, but she wasn't waiting for an answer. It hadn't been a question.

Once again, the Blue Room was empty of energy and reflections. Golden sunshine poured in through the windows, and when I opened the casings, a flowery scent, as if I was standing in a florist's shop, wafted inside. Hard to believe that this was the same room where the chaos had reigned last night.

I shrugged to myself. I'd long ago given up trying to understand how the energy and the reflections worked. It was better not to question too much.

Before I undressed, I peeked into the bathroom. If something or someone was in there, I didn't want to fumble with clothes before bolting from the room.

Nothing. Just a surprisingly modern room, as I'd noted the night before, with the huge bathtub-shower combination towering in the middle.

"Okay," I said out loud. Strangely, my voice echoing slightly in the marbled room gave me comfort. As if I was putting my own imprint on it. The bathroom, after all, was where Joelyn had disappeared in my reflection.

I turned the knob, and warm water fell from the oversized showerhead. The spray washed away the shock and strain of the morning and left just Joelyn. She had walked into this bathroom with such sad resolve. Something told me that she had come in with purpose and intent, and I wasn't sure it was a good one. Was Lauren dogged enough to uncover why? Or would a reflection pop up to give us the answer?

As I vaulted over the enormous tub lip, the mystery of Joelyn Steward seized me and wouldn't let go. Shit. I was as addicted to the mystery as much as Lauren was. The thrill of the unknown, the chase for answers, it was intoxicating.

Downstairs, the scent of breakfast greeted me even before I reached the kitchen. Jo stood at the stove, pouring beaten eggs into a pan. She moved with quiet confidence, her motions as precise as everything about her.

"I hope you eat eggs," she said without turning around.

"I do." A thrill ran through me. She knew it was me without even looking. Was she noticing me too? I was so out of practice navigating this first flush of attraction. Something thrilling and terrifying all at once.

"Good. They're French omelets, if that's also okay."

"I wouldn't know French from Russian or American."

She laughed lightly. "Russian ones usually have potatoes and sour cream and maybe some scallions. French are all about the eggs. Nothing else. Cooked just enough on the outside and a core of soft scrambled goodness on the inside."

She rolled the completed omelet out of the pan and onto a china plate already on the kitchen island. With a swipe of a knife, she cut the omelet neatly in two and slid one half on a plate to me. "Eat while it's hot."

"Shouldn't we wait for Lauren?"

"Oh, she treats her morning ritual like a spa day. It could be a while."

I used the back of my fork to cut a piece. The fresh and buttery scent made my mouth water. I was hungry.

"Stop. Wait." She whirled to the fridge. "I forgot the cheese." A moment later, she dabbed soft herbed cheese on our plates. "Not truly authentic but super good if you want."

I took a bite. "Mm," I said my mouth full. "I didn't know I wanted it until I tasted it."

We ate in almost comfortable silence for a beat, but I began to wish that Lauren with her incessant chatter was here. I dug around for something to say. "Do you have any new prospects?" I winced. "I mean, for a new job?" Shit, I was making her sound desperate both romantically and professionally.

"No, not really. I connected with an old professor at Berkeley last month, and I'm translating his findings on plasma energy into French and Japanese for fun. We both agree it's important to make scientific knowledge accessible globally, not only to English speakers and readers."

"French and Japanese?" Jo was certainly full of surprises.

"Yeah, I used to translate all sorts of articles between college and grad school."

"Don't let her downplay that. I told you, Jo is a genius." Lauren waltzed into the kitchen. She was dressed in very expensive but casual clothes. I'd seen enough of the same kind on Keera. Enough to know that a hoodie wasn't always just a hoodie. "She taught herself hieroglyphs when she was in middle school."

"I only read and write Japanese,."

"Still impressive," I said.

"My mom is French, so I grew up bilingual. So it doesn't count."

"Yeah, but Japanese does. You learned that in, what, a year over there?"

"My biggest fan." She smiled indulgently at Lauren. "English can't be the gatekeeper for scientific conversation, and the University of Tokyo was doing some interesting things in particle physics."

"Wow." Jo was beginning to sound out-of-my-league impressive.

"But I got so lonely, which is weird because personal space is way less over there. Strangers stand too close for this American."

"I flew over to crowd her a little more," Lauren said. "It was great. We went on adventures and ate some great food. She can't get rid of me now. I show up like a bad penny wherever she ends up."

"Don't ever stop."

"Fat chance."

Their easy banter gave me a glimpse into what their normal was. From the outside, it looked pretty great. Like a song they knew by heart always playing in the background. My life had never had that kind of rhythm. The reflections constantly threw everything off beat.

Later, when Lauren popped the last bite of her omelet into her mouth, she leaned back on her stool. "Okay, so how are we going to break into the wall upstairs?"

"I was wondering when you'd get to that," Jo said softly.

"You're not going to fight it?"

"Would it work?"

Lauren shook her head. "How else are we going to find the box?"

"I know we're going to have to see this through before you'll drop it. I still don't believe any of this, no offense." This part was addressed to me. "I'll take it through banging holes in the wall, and then, it's over. Okay?"

Lauren tilted her head from side to side. "Okay."

"Seriously. This can't become one of your I-won't-let-it-go obsessions."

"Okay." She sighed with fake annoyance and a real smile. "Let's go get a hammer from the garage." She got up to put her plan into action.

Jo grabbed her arm gently. "Wait. I already called Leo. We need a professional."

"Oh my God. Really?"

"Yes, he's coming over tomorrow. Early."

Lauren scooted around the island and grabbed Jo in a brief hug.

"Thanks. You're the best." She stepped back and turned to me. "You're staying, of course. At least one more night?"

"We can't ask her to stay forever." Not quite the response I wanted from Jo.

"She wants to know what's in the box as much as we do."

I did. Curiosity had its hooks in me. But I wasn't ready to overstay my welcome, especially if Jo wasn't going to support it. I took the coward's way out. I didn't answer.

"We can't do this without you," Lauren said simply. "So you're staying, right?"

Another day would keep me off Keera's radar until I could figure out what to tell her about New York and beyond. Staying would also keep me on Jo's radar. I wasn't sure yet if that was a good thing or not.

The safe choice would have been to leave before I wore out my welcome, before I got too tangled up in something that wasn't mine to hold on to. But the pull of the mystery—and Jo—made it hard to walk away. "I'd kind of like to see if there's anything up there."

Lauren whooped, and Jo remained silent, biting her lower lip. What was she thinking? I studied her face, desperate for a tell, but she was unreadable.

The vibe was awkward, the air thick with unspoken words. Jo and I seemed equally self-conscious, while Lauren glanced back and forth between us with an amused, knowing expression. "I'm going back to the study to see if I can find anything else about this long-lost aunt. Jo, weren't you going kayaking this afternoon? Take Hazel, she'll love it."

"Um, I was thinking about it."

Lauren let out a breath, exasperated. "Ask her, Jo. You can make a pact not to talk about the reflections and the energy."

And when Jo said nothing, Lauren turned to me. "Hazel, do you want to go? It's fun."

"I've never been," I confessed. It was an easy out. I'd spent the last twelve hours wondering and fantasizing about Jo, but this new reality of us spending the entire afternoon together was turning a little fast for me. I would be in the center of her radar.

"That doesn't matter. Jo's a great teacher. You can use my boat, and the river's gorgeous this time of year."

"Do you mind?" I made my decision.

"No," Jo said simply. Too simple to read if she was being forced into babysitting or actually okay with this impromptu date. *What the hell. Go for it.* By the end of the afternoon, maybe I'd know if I was having real feelings for her or just a knee-jerk reaction to my fight with Keera and Jo's sweet rescue this morning.

She cleared her throat. "I have to send a few emails to my old professor, and then we can go?"

"Great." Lauren bounced through the door. "I'll leave some shorts and kayak stuff on your bed upstairs, Hazel. Come up whenever you're ready." And then she was gone.

My phone buzzed in my jeans pocket. "I've got a few things to take care of myself." I had no idea who it was, but I didn't want Jo to think I was idle. She was so accomplished.

She nodded as if convincing herself that we were doing this. "Take it out in the garden. I don't know why, but the reception is better out there. Give me an hour or so?"

"Of course. Take as much time as you need."

Was this a date or not? Time would tell.

The garden that I'd only glimpsed through windows and French doors was breathtaking in person. A full-on English garden, with gravel paths winding between water features and some of the healthiest plants I'd ever seen. Hanging fuchsia baskets were bursts of pink and purple and marked the route to a bench in the center. I sat under a wooden pergola and pulled out my phone.

Is everything okay up there? The text was from Gran.

Yes. Why? I typed back.

The phone rang almost before I sent my reply. "Because," she began without a greeting, "Keera called and scared me half to death."

"You're shitting me." I couldn't believe she'd called Gran, but she knew that was the best way to get to me.

"I am not. She said you weren't responding to her texts. She had me half convinced that something horrible had happened to you. That I'd sent you into a murder den."

"I'm fine, Gran, but you're kind of right about the house. Listen to this." I told her everything. I downplayed the eroticism of the dream quite a bit, but she got the gist anyway. She listened without interruption until I told her we were on hold waiting for the handyman to break into the walls of the Blue Room.

"It sounds like you're taking control. That's good."

"That's not me. It's Lauren. She's one of the most proactive people I've ever met. Always moving forward at lightning speed. It's amazing and scary all at the same time."

"And Jo?"

"Oh, she's not a believer. But strangely, she may be open to it? Maybe at least a little bit. I don't know."

"And she's nice?"

It was an odd question. As I turned it over in my head, Gran added, "She's single, you know."

"Oh my God. Did you send me up here for her?"

"No, of course not. We've gone over this. These girls need help, but if you and Jo hit it off, that would be a nice bonus."

"Gran, I don't need or want any help with my love life."

"I beg to differ. When your love life calls and scares the bejeezus out of me, that tells me otherwise."

"I'm really sorry about that. But you know, Keera and I aren't together anymore."

"Maybe not romantically, sweetheart. In other ways, though…"

She wasn't wrong. She wasn't saying anything I hadn't thought repeatedly in the last twenty-four hours. If things were going to change, that was on me to make it happen.

"I hear you, Gran. I do."

"Good. I love you very much. Keep your eyes open. You'll never know what you could find up there."

"I love you too. Wait a sec, what does that mean?"

"You'll know when you see it. Bye, Hazel." She hung up. That settled it. I'd been sent to Meerblick to hunt for more than reflections.

THE LETTERS

The Past: Eliza

Dec 8, 1925

My love,
 Did your friend Jules say anything about our using her apartment last night? I know you thought that whopper I told her about needing a quiet place to work on a jazz song for Henry's band was completely transparent. You said she'd be sympathetic to our cause, but, Joelyn, I simply can't bear for anyone to know. On some level, you are right, I am not comfortable with what's between us. Every morning when I wake up, I am determined to overcome my sinful impulses, but come bedtime, I realize that you're all I've thought about all day. Thoughts of your touch are the only thing that can send me off to sleep. Besides, it's more than a little embarrassing the way Jules looks at us like she knows everything. The other reason I'd rather her not know what is going on in her own house is that I want to hold everything that is happening to us close to me. Close to my heart. I don't want to share you with anyone at all, even if it is only a word or a look or a thought.
 Is that too selfish?
 E

❖

December 13, 1925

Dear Joelyn,
 We may have to slow down a little. Mother came to my room last night as I was getting ready for bed and made yet another snide comment about my hair. Then we had what she called a loving heart-to-heart. More of a lecture, if you ask me, but what's important is what she said at the end. She started by telling me that people are talking about

your family. By people, she means the Littneys. They think
that your mother has gone too far this time by going to that
Chinese girl's wedding in that horrible Chinatown. She
asked me how your mother could consort with all those dirty
foreigners as if they were equals. It is not even appropriate
for your mother to try to get Chinese girls into schools rather
than keeping them at home to be first the property of their
fathers and then their husbands.

You know I completely disagree. As we have discussed,
all Americans should be equal. And here she felt compelled
to make another sly observation about how obeying one's
father is not necessarily a bad thing. She asked me why your
mother felt compelled to go to the wedding at all. She said
those people are not like us. They have different values that
will corrupt us if we get too close. Joelyn, I saw red, and I
shot back at her something like, you're right, Mother, they
are not like us at all. They have a deeper cultural connection
than we do, and they are richer than we are. I then told her
that the father of the bride was one of the foremost jewelers
in the city, and the groom's family owned a company larger
than Father's. She got all quiet and asked me how I knew so
much about it.

Stupid, stupid me. I didn't see what was coming and told
her that you had been there too. You said that the ceremony
was more lavish than any you had ever seen. That was when
the fireworks started. She said that no self-respecting mother
would let her unmarried daughter into a neighborhood that
had brothels, gambling halls, and opium dens, that you were
a bad influence, and that we had been seeing much too much
of each other. I started laughing and pointed out that in the
spring, she practically broke her arm throwing me at you at
the Woman's Athletic Club. I might have even used the word
hypocrite. It was her turn to laugh and to tell me that I was
too immature to understand how the world works. I told her
that I wasn't too young to understand how she could use your
family to get what she wanted and drop them when they were
no longer useful. It must have hit too close to home since she
got off my bed and stormed to the door, only to turn to tell me
this conversation was over if I couldn't behave civilly. Can
you believe she slammed the door on her way out? Who's

immature now? I yelled that I would never stop seeing you. That was last night, and she has avoided me all day today. I am not going to apologize, and I am not going to stop seeing you.

All my love,
E

❖

December 15, 1925

I'll have to sneak out and cover up the fact that I am gone. I will see you at Jules's at 8:00.

CHAPTER EIGHT

The Present: Hazel

My resolve to finally deal with the Keera situation grew as I climbed the stairs to the Blue Room. Lauren, as good as her word, had laid out a bright blue rash guard and a pair of matching swim trunks on the bed. I ran my fingers across the rough, waterproof Lycra. I eyed the clothes with suspicion. Dang, how wet was I going to get? And they looked smaller than I liked. They would fit me like a glove.

Oh no.

Was Lauren also part of this ridiculous romantic setup? She had practically pushed me into the boat this morning. And last night she had told me as such. *I like the way Jo is when she is with you.* It hadn't read romantic at the time, more family concern, but looking back at the statement, maybe it had carried a different intention.

I didn't like being manipulated, but if everyone was pushing me in a certain direction, maybe it was time I took the reins myself. I drew my phone out of my back pocket and pulled up Keera's contact info. Once I tapped on it and said even half of what I wanted to, there was no going back.

Keera let it ring almost until it went to voice mail. "Yes?" Her tone was curt. She had already decided to be annoyed.

"Next time you want to get ahold of me, please leave my grandmother out of it." I skipped the pleasantries too.

"You weren't answering my texts."

"By design, Keera. I need a break."

"From what?" Her voice was icy but also genuinely confused. That was part of the problem, Keera never got when she pushed too far.

I paused and considered her question. "From everything. Mostly, I hate the celebrity shoots. I know we need them for cash flow, but I want to be the one who decides who we book. I'm through working with spoiled adults who treat their animal companions like props."

Silence buzzed out of the phone. In the past, I would've caved quickly, too scared of the fallout. But not this time. A door to my frustration had been cracked open in the last few days. Now, it swung wide on its rusty hinges.

"I'm serious, Keera. I hope you're hearing me."

"I am."

"Good."

"And we'll seriously talk about it when we get back from New York."

Heat flushed through my body as anger bubbled up in my chest. "Don't you get it? I'm not going to New York."

On the other end, she exhaled sharply, as if dealing with a petulant child. "I wish you would reconsider. That puts me in a very uncomfortable position with Caleb and his manager."

I shrugged even though she couldn't see me. "That's your problem."

"I told them we'd fly in tonight."

"I guess you're going to have to un-tell them, then."

"You don't understand. I don't care about the money, well, I do, but not as much as I care about our reputation. In the end, we must protect our position no matter the cost."

"That does make sense."

"Thank you." I could almost see the smirk on her face. She thought she had won.

"May I suggest, next time, don't agree to a deal until you've checked with me first. I'll be back in the gallery in two days at the earliest. Just to let you know in case any other offers come in."

She drew in a quick, sharp breath. And there it was. This door could never be closed.

"Please don't contact me," I added for good measure, "until I see you in person. Good-bye, Keera." I hung up and stared at the phone, half expecting it to explode in protest.

Sure, there would be consequences, but I could kick those down the road a couple of days and relax into the moment. I texted Gran to tell her that I'd be offline for the afternoon and tossed the phone onto the bed. It bounced on the plush bedspread and lay silently. I took in a deep breath.

❖

"I've never seen the water so calm." We floated in the greenish flatwater of the Gualala River under the afternoon sun. "Usually, the wind comes up in the afternoon. We're lucky."

Jo paddled effortlessly upriver in a sleek red kayak. If it had wheels, it would have been a race car. I jerked along beside her in Lauren's beginner boat, as Jo had called it. Bright orange, short, and wide: Jo had cheerfully described it as easy to steer and super stable.

I begged to differ. First, I'd balked when she'd wanted me to stuff my body into a cockpit half my size. Jo had talked me down, patiently pointing where to put my feet, legs, and torso. Then, as soon as we'd launched, I'd almost flipped it twice. Jo had been right there to steady the boat, saving me from a dunking in the cold river.

Now I'd almost gotten the hang of it. I reached out with my paddle to catch the water beside me.

"Use your core and not your arms. Yes, that's good. Feels better, doesn't it?" Jo encouraged me.

It did, and not only because my forearms instantly stopped screaming in pain. Mostly, it was because we were splashing deeper into the magnificent redwood forest and farther away from my normal life. With each stroke, I breathed a little easier.

She identified the big white birds as egrets and the darker ones as great blue herons. At one point, she swore she spotted a river otter. We floated silently for many minutes, but I never saw it.

Around one bend, a massive oak tree shaded the water below its sprawling branches. Jo angled her kayak so she faced me. "Right here is Jack London's favorite fishing hole. The water gets deeper, so the fish stop to rest."

"Jack London the author? The guy who wrote *Call of the Wild*?"

"Yep, toward the end of his life, he moved out here to get away from it all. Fun fact, his mom believed in all the stuff you do. She gave séances in the city. Or at least, that's what my middle school English teacher told us." Jo grabbed my boat so we wouldn't crash into each other. Her hand was barely inches from mine.

"I don't believe I can talk to the dead," I said softly. "And they're memories, not live reenactments."

"I guess that's fair." We floated side by side, close enough that my pulse quickened. She reached across my kayak to point at the bank, dense with vegetation. "During Prohibition, the mob had a hideout right there. And the Pomo Native Americans have walked this river for almost twelve thousand years. I guess there're memories everywhere, even if we can't see them."

"Exactly." Was she coming around? "That's why I love what I do. A photograph frames the world around us and creates a story tied to a single moment. It's a reflection that everyone can see, and it lets me connect with things that otherwise might go unnoticed."

She nodded her gaze distant as she processed my words. "That makes sense, but it's a big jump to seeing the reflections."

I shrugged and almost flipped the boat. Stable my ass. "Not really. There are a lot of things you have to take on faith. This isn't the usual kind, but it doesn't mean it's not true. In the end, people simply have to believe me."

Jo studied me in that inscrutable way of hers. She tugged at her life jacket as if it was too tight. "I believe that you believe," she said with a tense smile that relaxed into something more natural. "I'm surprised myself. It's a start, right?"

"It is. Thank you." I placed my palm against my chest in gratitude and almost dropped my paddle in the river in the process.

"Careful," Jo teased. "It's a long swim back." She laughed and broke through the last of my tension.

From there, our conversation flowed as easily as the river. I described the awful photographs, one blurry flower after another, I had taken as a kid after my grandmother had given me my first digital camera, the Canon PowerShot. She told me about floating down the Dordogne River in France as a child. That was where she'd fallen in love with kayaking. We bonded over stories of childhood dogs. Atticus for me. D'Artagnan for her. We both liked that the names came from books. When we finally pulled the boats off the river, my fate was sealed. I liked this woman. A lot.

Lauren and Edgar popped out to the porch as we drove up. Edgar happily bounded over, his tail wagging a mile a minute. He greeted Jo and then me, stuffing his nose into my hand as if to say, *Welcome to the family.*

"Have fun?" Lauren asked, fixing both Jo and me with pointed looks.

"We did," Jo said, simply grabbing a kayak strap on the top of the car. "Give us a hand, Ren. These things feel twice as heavy at the end of the paddle."

Lauren jumped to Jo's side, and the real question was lost as we manhandled the boats down from the racks and into a nearby shed.

Once the boats were safely stored, Jo patted Lauren on the back. "Thanks. I'm going to take a shower. Can you pull the chicken out of the freezer? Maybe we'll roast it."

"I don't want you to cook for me," I jumped in. "Is there takeout nearby? I can go grab something."

"That's a sweet offer." Jo's appreciative glance raised goose bumps on my arms. "There's nothing nearby except a great bakery that's closed now. Town is, like, thirty minutes away. This is simple. No worries."

She smiled, gave a little wave, and glided up the stairs with her remarkable grace. I blew out a quick breath and ducked my head to the inevitable. *Oh no. This is really happening. At least on my end.*

"So." Lauren flashed me a knowing smile. "You did have fun." Was she in cahoots with Gran? I was beginning to see what the formable Clarissa had given to each of her four-greats granddaughters.

Normally, I would bristle at such interference, but honestly? This time, I didn't mind. It felt less like being pushed and more like being seen. "I did," I said simply, and that seemed to satisfy her.

I entertained myself until dinner by changing out of the skintight kayak gear, grabbing my camera, and heading back outside. The second my hands closed on the lens, my whole body tingled with the connection. I couldn't remember the last time I'd taken a full day off from shooting.

The backyard of Meerblick was a stunning canvas: a wild craggy bluff that tumbled into the ocean. I'd seen the phenomenal view from the house, but standing here now, with nothing between me and the sea, my experience was raw and untouched. The golden hour was close, the time right before sunset when the light was redder and softer than earlier in the day. No color correction done later on a computer would even come close. The golden hour was the real magic of photography.

I snapped a few pictures of the waves rolling into shore, trying to capture the power and beauty of the water. I failed miserably. Nice postcard shots, nothing more. So I focused my camera back on a small beach at the bottom of a private stairway. I recognized it as the setting of the picture with Joelyn, her family, and the other woman, Eliza. I dropped my lens and stared intently, hoping to see an echo of that day, but the reflections never came when I called them.

A sharp bark echoed behind me, and I spun to see Edgar peeping around a shrub, fixated on something in the distance. I adjusted the frame and shot quickly. The action brought a familiar, weightless flutter to my chest. A feeling I hadn't experienced in far too long. *I'm in the zone.*

Edgar and I wandered the bluff together, my camera capturing his every move. At one point, he jumped on a stone bench and stared directly at me and the lens. Our connection buzzed through me, spreading to my fingers. I couldn't hit the shutter fast enough.

For the first time in what felt like forever, I was having fun. This was what I should have been feeling on every shoot: alive, invigorated, and connected. Keera always said she understood my passion, but she never truly got it.

Edgar jumped off the bench and ran to the bluff, chasing a seagull he'd never catch. As I raised my camera, he whipped around to focus on something over my shoulder. His whole expression transformed into one so full of love and devotion, I shot first and looked second.

Jo stood on the back porch. Her dark hair was still wet from the shower, and she wore jeans and a blue Berkeley hoodie. My stomach clenched. She could've been watching the whole time. Feeling awkward, I gave a small wave.

"I hope you don't mind," I said when we were close enough. "I was taking some pictures of Edgar."

"No, that's terrific. I'd love to see them."

"Of course. I'll print out the best ones for you back at my gallery." As soon as I said it, I realized that without knowing it, I'd devised a surefire way to see her again. Happy accident or shameless plotting? I was as bad as Lauren and my grandmother.

"Okay," she said, giving no clue if this was welcome or not. Edgar jumped up on her, and she pushed him gently to the ground. "Down, Edgar. Oh my God, he never does that."

"He's happy to see you."

"Or maybe he's ready to eat. How about you?"

"I am. That was a lot of exercise for me today." I dropped a hand to my stomach. "I'm already sore."

Jo's gaze drifted down my body, lingering here and there, finally settling on my hand at my belly button. "A nice hot bath after dinner might help. You could go for a swim in that bathtub of yours."

I choked back a groan. The image of Jo and me, limbs tangled in a hot bath, rose in my mind. Of course, that hadn't been an invitation.

After dinner, Lauren confessed that she'd poked around in the study all afternoon, hoping to find more information on Joelyn. "Grandpa's system of cataloging is so complicated, but once I got the hang of it, oh my God, it's brilliant. Flat-out ingenious."

"OCD," Jo mouthed to me when Lauren wasn't looking.

"I loved rummaging around in his mind, getting to know him better. He's been gone for a while now, but we reconnected this afternoon. It's almost like I can see reflections now too." She looked at me as if waiting for confirmation and seeking validation.

"You're right. There are lots of ways to connect with memories."

Lauren lit up as if I'd invited her into a secret organization she had always known existed. "I was only half-successful. I didn't find anything more about our girl. It was like someone had systematically gone through the archive and gotten rid of any mention of her. It's weird. I found tons of pictures of Helen and Lewis. But not one more of Joelyn. We're lucky someone misfiled the one I found."

"Did someone have a vendetta or something against her?" I asked. "It's a mystery for sure."

"Only until tomorrow morning. This is so exciting. There's going to be something in that box that will tell us what happened."

My stomach sank. I raised my coffee mug to my lips, letting the bitter aroma fill my senses as I weighed how to break her optimism gently. "Lauren, you do know that we may not even find the box?"

"What?" The color drained from her face. Shit. She was even more invested than I'd realized. She stared at me wide-eyed, and the weight of her immense expectations settled heavily on my shoulders.

"I mean," I quickly added, "I definitely saw Joelyn put that box in the wall. No question there."

Lauren's fingers trembled as she pressed them to her lips. She so badly wanted to have faith in me and trust my gift.

"But," I continued, "we have no idea what happened next. She could've come back a minute or a day later and taken it out. Or workmen could've remodeled the room decades ago, and the box could've been destroyed. There's no way for us to know."

"No." Lauren shook her head. "It will be there."

Jo reached over and put a comforting hand on her arm. "Hazel's preparing us for all the possibilities." She raised her eyebrows at me, begging me to play along. "She's being realistic. We all need to be."

I reached out a comforting hand to her other arm. "What I saw did happen one hundred years ago."

Lauren shrugged us both off. "We'll find something there tomorrow. You'll see." Her voice brimmed with determination, her version of realism.

The idea of not finding the box was a buzzkill, and the conversation stalled. Putting distance between her expectations and ours, Lauren gathered the dishes and brought them to the sink.

I rose to help when Jo held me back. "Doing something is her way of dealing with the potential of disappointment."

"I didn't mean to—"

"No. No. It's good. She needs to mentally prepare for the moment if there's nothing up there."

If.

It wasn't just the word but the way she said it. Soft. Careful. Like belief was slipping in around the edges of her doubt. And somehow, that made my hope bloom sharper. Not just about what we might find upstairs, but about her and whatever might be building between us.

"You can head up to bed if you're tired," she said softly.

I was. Between not sleeping last night and more exercise today than five gym visits, I could've put my head down on the table like a toddler.

"That would be great."

"I'm taking Hazel up to bed," Jo announced.

Lauren must've still been mentally preparing. She didn't react at all.

I did, though. A quick jolt in my chest, and my heart began to thud in my ears. I was still tried, exhausted even, but now it hummed beneath a sharper question. What would happen in a bed with Jo?

Seemingly flustered, Jo quickly backtracked. "I mean, she's going upstairs so she can sleep."

"I knew what you meant." I smiled, trying to smooth the moment over. And I did, but that didn't chase away the image of us in bed that had lodged in my mind.

Jo trotted up the stairs ahead of me and didn't stop until we were standing outside the Blue Room. Her fingers hovered uncertainly over the brass doorknob, hesitating before she turned it. The door swung open with a soft creak. Neither of us stepped inside.

"I had fun today," I said, my voice steadier than I was. My eyes sought hers, searching for a flicker of the connection I'd felt all day. I knew we weren't going inside together. She had totally misspoken downstairs, but maybe the evening wasn't completely over?

"I did too." Her hand drifted to the nape of her neck. Her gaze met mine, a mixture of warmth and uncertainty in her eyes. It lingered until she said, "Good night, Hazel. I hope it's an easy one."

Her smile was fleeting, barely touching her lips before fading. She turned and strode down the hall, her footsteps silent on the thick carpet.

Dang. That could've gone better. Another gentle squeeze of my arm or a little stronger endorsement of the day. Anything to suggest that I wasn't the only one feeling this spark.

But as quickly as those thoughts surfaced, they were overshadowed by a creeping unease. My attention snapped to the room before me, its presence suddenly oppressive. I didn't want to go in.

At the end of the hall, Jo reappeared, her lips parted as if she was about to say something. The moment she saw me frozen in place, uncertainty clouded her expression. "You okay?"

"I'm not sure." My voice wavered. I bit my lip. "I think I'm nervous about sleeping in there again."

"Sorry, I should've thought of that." Her expression softened as she stepped closer, finally wrapping her gentle fingers around my elbow. Her warm touch grounded me, and I felt better.

"Let's go in together?" she asked.

"Please." I took a deep breath, and we crossed the threshold almost side by side.

Jo flipped on the light and scanned the still dark corners of the Blue Room. "Anything?"

"No." Like this morning, the room was empty, but still, I hugged myself tightly to ward off any energy lurking in the shadows.

Her brow furrowed with concern. "Do you want to sleep in another room?"

Relief surged through me. "Oh my God, can I?"

"Sure. No problem."

We moved into another wing of the house. "This is where the family has always slept. The Blue Room is in the guest wing."

I glanced at the row of doors on either side, each one possibly hiding more reflections. "Geez, how many bedrooms are there?"

"Way too many for two women hiding from the world. Here."

She opened the last door on the right. "This was Clarissa's room back in the day."

She flipped a switch, and a delicate chandelier, its crystals twinkling like stars, lit up the room. A grand four-poster bed, its wooden frame intricately carved with flowers, stood against one wall. Across from it, a vanity with a large, gilded mirror gleamed. Its surface was cluttered with perfume bottles and silver-handled brushes, as if Clarissa had just walked away. Every detail— the rich fabrics, the polished wood, the elegant accessories—wove a picture of refined comfort. It occurred to me that the room, preserved like a museum from another time, was also a type of reflection.

"Are all the rooms this amazing?" I asked, taking it in.

"No, not in this wing. Mine has posters of the women from *Firefly* on two walls. God, I loved that show a little too much, if you know what I mean." A faint flush rose in her cheeks.

I grinned. I understood completely. My high school crushes had revolved around Piper Perabo and *Imagine Me and You*.

Jo turned on what looked like a vintage Tiffany lamp on the nightside table. Its floral design echoed those on the bedframe. "We've kept Clarissa's as she would have. I hope that doesn't trigger anything for you."

I glanced around. The room was calm and empty, but that didn't mean anything. "Nothing so far. This is much better. Thank you."

"Bathroom's through there, and the bed should be made. We just had a cleaning crew out here." She pulled down the comforter to reveal crisp white sheets. "Great. It is. Both Lauren and I'll be right down the hall if you need us."

"Thank you," I said again. "I know I've been a lot of trouble."

She smiled softly, her eyes sparkling with warmth. "No, Lauren's got that covered. Honestly, I had more fun today than I've had in a while. I should be thanking you."

Her gaze lingered, and she stepped closer. Her hand found my shoulder, resting there gently. The simple touch sent shivers down my arm. This was a much better good night. Would it lead to a full hug that would lead to a movie-perfect kiss which would lead to...

She continued to stare, her eyes never leaving mine. "I...I..." she began and maddeningly let her thought trail off. Pain flickered in her eyes, and she closed them and herself to whatever might've come next. "Hope you sleep well." And then, she was gone.

I stood there alone, my heart still racing and my thoughts spinning down a path I'd probably never walk. If nothing else, Jo had reminded me that there could be a romantic life after Keera. Whether she'd be a part of it or not, I'd go home and take control of both my professional and personal life.

I got into bed with a lighter heart and fell almost immediately into a deep and dreamless sleep.

I jolted awake to see a reflection hovering at the edge of the bed. This time, it wasn't Joelyn. Instead, an older woman with the unmistakable dark coloring of the Steward women stood before me. Her head tilted imperiously, radiating withering judgment. I glanced opposite her, hoping to see the target of her disdain, but the room was empty. Only one person, one memory ever came through at a time with these usual reflections.

This was Clarissa. I recognized her from the pictures. Her face was contorted into a scowl, her mouth so pinched, it almost disappeared. Whatever the unseen person was saying wasn't sitting well with her.

Fully alert, I sat up to get a better view, praying that her actions would bring clarity to whatever had gone on in this house. Breakfast would be so much more fun if I could serve up a mystery-busting story with coffee.

Clarissa shook her head and thrust out thick parchment papers covered in blue ink. She shook the papers furiously, her sharp, angry eyes fixed on her companion.

She jabbed an accusatory finger into the empty space, said something lost to the silent past, and then flung the papers at the invisible person with an impressive sweep of her arm. Once she let them go, they flew beyond the energy ball that held the memory and blinked out of existence. Even a century later, it played dramatically.

Clarissa jabbed her finger again, this time waiting for a response. Her gaze grew cold and flinty, as if she didn't like what she heard. She turned her head to the door. I followed her gaze, desperately hoping to catch a glimpse of someone else from the past. Who was leaving the room? What were the papers?

Nothing. The maddening limits of this gift were on full display in this reflection.

The fight drained out of her, Clarissa bowed her head in obvious defeat. When she raised her head, her expression had softened into worry. And then she flickered and vanished entirely.

I sank back into the pillows as I took stock of myself. I was fine. This was a typical run-of-the-mill reflection. No erratic energy crackled around me. I wasn't entangled with it. I was an observer like I normally was.

Somewhere off in the distance, Edgar started barking. His sharp yips grew louder until he was right outside the door.

"Is everything all right in there?" Jo's soft voice came through the door.

I lay in bed still processing.

"Hazel?" Her concern was unmistakable.

"Yes, I'm fine. Come in."

Edgar trotted in first, head to the ground like a bloodhound. He methodically poked his nose into corners and under the bed until he reached the exact spot where Clarissa had stood. He froze there, sniffing intently at something only he could detect.

Jo caught on. "Oh no. Something else happened. Didn't it?"

I nodded.

"You look okay."

I nodded again.

"What's he doing?" she asked, returning her attention to Edgar.

"I wish I knew. Believe me, I really do."

"He knows something," she mused. "I've read articles that say dogs can sense earthquakes before they strike. There's even one that suggests it's the changes in electrical fields or the ionization of air at pressurized rock surfaces. There's some science behind this."

We both focused on Edgar, who sat alertly in place, ears perked, listening for God knew what. With the same effortless grace she always had, Jo moved to the bed and slid across the covers to sit cross-legged at its foot. "You better tell me what *this* is, though."

Who the hell looks this good in the morning? She wore tank top pajamas with matching shorts. They were as formfitting as her running clothes the day before. On anyone else, they would have been an outfit and not something to sleep in. More significantly, they highlighted that her tight, athletic body was only a couple of feet away from me, leaning closer to hear what I might say.

I resisted the urge to smooth down my hair. "I saw Clarissa and someone fighting. Joelyn, I think, for some reason." I tried to paint the reflection as I'd seen it. I wanted to bring her into my world. I didn't want that curiosity shining in her eyes to fade. "For sure, they were arguing over the papers that Clarissa was holding," I finished.

"But you never actually saw Joelyn?"

"No. I've nothing to back it up. It's only a feeling."

"It's a solid theory." She nodded to herself. "Clarissa was a true matriarch, a real force of nature in all the family stories. If you buy all this, it absolutely makes sense that she's running the show."

"Do you? Buy all this?"

She glanced at Edgar, who still kept watch and then met my gaze. "Maybe. I don't know."

I reached out with a light touch to her arm. "I'll take that."

"Ooh. What have we here?"

Lauren stood at the open door, a shit-eating grin spread across her face.

Jo jumped off the bed as if Lauren had caught us in flagrante. Heat radiated off my face like a furnace. Meanwhile, Edgar stayed rooted to his spot a couple of feet away. She turned her attention to him, looking at him for the first time.

"Oh my God." She flung her hands into the air dramatically. "I missed another one, didn't I?" These Steward women were quick on the uptake.

"To be fair," Jo said, "I missed it too. Edgar sensed something, though. He started barking, and now he's on guard or something."

Without hesitation, Lauren climbed onto the bed, planting herself exactly where Jo had been moments before. "Tell me everything."

I did. For this second time, I tried to stick to the facts. But Lauren was worse, or better, at spinning them into her own theory.

"Of course it was Joelyn. And those papers? Could they have been a will? People fight about wills all the time."

"Maybe," I said, "but why would Clarissa have thrown her will at her daughter?"

Lauren nodded. "You think whatever they were, they were Joelyn's?"

They both looked at me for an answer. I shrugged, which was becoming my default reaction.

"Maybe we'll know in a couple of hours when Leo comes," Lauren answered her own question and bounced in place with anticipation.

I waited for Jo's usual rebuttal, her voice of reason cutting through Lauren's enthusiasm. It didn't come. Instead, she tilted her head back and forth as she rubbed Edgar's head.

Hot damn. She might not admit it, but she was excited too.

THE LETTERS

The Past: Eliza

Dec 18, 1925

Sweetheart,

You must believe me when I tell you that I want to spend Christmas with you, but I cannot tell Father that I want to go to your house. They are suspicious. I see it in their glances and hear it in their whispers when they think I am not paying attention. Mother even remarked to Father that I was too emotional during our heart-to-heart. Goodness help me. The servants are looking at me differently too. Robert practically spits out, "Yes, miss," when I hand him a letter and an order for your house. Do you think there is some way he is reading them? Joelyn, the thought has me in knots. I know you told me to be calm. I tried but failed.

How are you so composed when the walls feel like they're closing in? I cannot imagine what will happen if we are found out, and then I think about keeping it a secret for the rest of our lives. I know the alternative is not one I can accept. I broke it off once between us, and it nearly killed me. So we must spend this Christmas and many more Christmases together. Love will find a way, right?

I have a little something wrapped for you sitting at the edge of my bedside table.

Forever Yours,
Eliza

❖

December 22, 1925

My love,

My parents have been invited over to the Littneys' for Christmas Dinner. I'll beg off, feigning a headache, and will be waiting for you in our parlor at eight. It will be perfect. All the servants will be out, and the house will be ours. What can go wrong?

Until Christmas,

E

CHAPTER NINE

The Present: Hazel

We spent the morning in the garden drinking way too many emotional support lattes, as both Lauren and Jo called them. The house thankfully had an endless supply of organic coffee. Lauren spun new theories with each steaming cup. About the fight. About what might be hidden in the wall. About why Joelyn had been *disappeared* from the family record. Lauren was like her own comedy podcast, sweeping us into her narrative until she hit us with some sharp, clever observation at the end.

It was a strange situation, trying to piece together a mystery from fragments only I could see. But wasn't that what we all did in life? Stumbled forward with only a fraction of the facts, making up stories to fill in the blanks. What did that strange look from someone mean? Or why didn't I get the promotion? In the end, weren't we all unreliable narrators of our own lives?

These reflections, however, felt fundamentally different. If they were someone's memories, why didn't I see them through the storyteller's eyes? Instead, it was as if the universe itself was the cinematographer, capturing these moments exactly as they happened. No ego. No self-deception or embellishment. No carefully curated version of the events. Just raw emotion playing out forever.

The idea of an unvarnished truth scared me. But there was a comfort too. On some level, it was nice to know that the whole story might be out there somewhere.

The doorbell rang, and Lauren bolted out of the room like a racehorse at the Kentucky Derby. "Leo's here."

The handyman could've stepped straight off the set of a home renovation show. His tight T-shirt showcased a build that said he lifted more than hammers, and his easy smile immediately put me at ease.

"What's this about banging a hole in the wall of this gorgeous house?"

"It's complicated." Jo pulled him in for a quick hug. "Leo, this is our friend, Hazel."

"It's not complicated at all," Lauren said. "We think something may be in the wall of the Blue Room, and we want to find out what it is."

If Leo thought the statement odd, he didn't bat an eye. He seemed to know the house well and, carrying a big toolbox, led the way to the Blue Room. "Which wall?" he asked once we were inside.

Both Jo and Lauren looked at me, and Leo, seemingly surprised for the first time, furrowed his brow.

"That one." I pointed to the wall across from the bed near the built-in closet. The one where Lauren had put the big black X.

"Okay." Leo slid his professional mask on and pulled a drop cloth and a handsaw out of his toolbox. He carefully positioned the drop cloth on the floor. "These old plaster walls can be messy. X marks the spot?"

This time, all three of them turned to me, full of expectation. Even Jo looked at me with hope and trust. My chest tightened. They all thought I knew what I was doing. With that criteria, I was a complete imposter.

"Yes." I approached and tapped the wall, praying that I'd remembered it correctly.

Leo went to work, sliding the saw into the wall, and with some effort and not so much mess, he cut a hole through the plaster and the wood lath underneath. When he was done, Lauren crept forward and clicked a flashlight on. As soon as Leo removed the plaster piece, she thrust the light into the cavity.

"Anything?" Jo's voice was soft with excitement.

"No," Lauren said flatly.

"Put the light over there. To the right," Leo directed her. "What are we looking for anyway?"

"A box," she answered.

"Shiny, silver, about this big." I palmed an imaginary box the size of a children's shoe box in the air.

"What do you see in there?" Jo squeezed in between them and took the flashlight from Lauren. After a minute, she handed it off to me. "You look."

I peered into the hole and flashed the light around. All I saw was space between the walls and a boatload of nothing. The box wasn't there. I pretended to look some more, but really, I didn't want to turn around and meet Jo's eyes.

"Maybe it was more toward the closet?" I heard the doubt in my voice.

"You want me to cut another hole?" Leo asked. The doubt was there too.

Silence hung heavy in the room, and then Jo said, "Yes. One more."

Leo slipped into the gap and cut a second hole on the other side of the stud from the first one. Lauren, her face tight with concentration, flashed the light into every nook and cranny.

"Nothing." Her voice was thick with disappointment.

I turned toward Jo. She mirrored Lauren's disillusionment, her lips pressed into a tight grimace, as if she was biting back every comment popping into her head.

"Sorry," I mouthed silently.

She winced. Seriously, it was as if I'd physically touched her.

"I got some patching plaster and all the other stuff in the truck. Want me to get it?"

"Yes," Jo said.

Something hard and flinty, a lot like what I'd seen in Clarissa's look that morning, settled over Jo's face. Dammit. All that progress we'd made, was it lost?

Leo was on his way out the door when Lauren, who still had the flashlight inside the wall, said, "Hey, how far does that part go?"

Lauren pointed the light at the back of the wall inside so we could all see. "Doesn't this look bigger from the outside than it does in here?"

Leo peered into the hole. "Could be. Maybe there's a double wall in there."

Lauren straightened. "We need to cut into it." She quickly assessed the situation.

Jo bristled. "Let's not add another hole we'll have to patch."

"What's one more hole?" Ignoring her, Lauren opened the closet door for Leo. "Can you get in there?"

"Of course. Same height?" Leo was already pulling his saw back out.

"Yes." Lauren took complete control. Jo and I hung back silently, probably for very different reasons. Me: failure. Her: frustration. Either way, the air hung heavy between us.

Cutting the new hole was slow work in the tight space. I could feel Jo tighten beside me with each push of the blade. At one point, she even shuffled over to put more space between us.

When Leo finally cut through, Lauren squeezed past him, her flashlight already searching. She passed back the piece of the wall and waved it around until Jo reluctantly grabbed it.

"I knew it. There's a double wall. I told you."

"There's nothing in here, Lauren." Leo eased out.

Undeterred, she continued to hunt with the light and her incredible single-mindedness.

Jo, on the other hand, had reached her limit. She stared at her feet while slowly shaking her head. I didn't need to see her face to know that defeat was written all over it.

That was that. I'd pack and get out of here as quickly as possible. It was going to be a long ride home with shame and failure as my passengers.

"What is that?" Lauren squealed.

Leo plunged his arms back into the tiny opening, grunting as he worked to extract something. Finally, he yanked the box from the wall. It was dusty and dull, coated in decades of neglect, but there was no mistake. It was the same box I'd seen in my reflection.

Lauren nearly snatched it out of his hands and rushed it to the bed. We all crowded around. Even Leo, now fully caught up in the adventure, leaned in. Reverently, Lauren brushed away the dust, revealing an embossed image of two lovers sitting under palm trees on its top.

She fingered the simple latch below, and her hand froze. "You open it, Jo."

"No." She hung back. "I'd have given up two holes ago. You made this happen, Lauren. You open it."

Lauren didn't need to be told twice. With a flick of her wrist, the lid swung open with a tiny pop. Instantly, Lauren's expression turned from delight to confusion.

"What is it?" Jo asked.

"I don't know." Lauren swung the opened box to me so I could see inside.

"Treasure?" Leo asked hopefully.

"Better," I said as the tension fell from my body, and a triumphant warmth surged inside me.

Inside were the papers that Clarissa had been wielding this

morning and decades before. Fine writing in blue ink on thick paper. Pages and pages of them, tied neatly, secured with a red ribbon.

"They're letters." I swiveled the box, still in Lauren's hands, so Jo could see.

She stared deep inside, noting every detail, but didn't raise her head to meet my gaze. This should have been the moment when, either by look or words, she'd tell me she believed that the reflections were real and not some *attention grab*, Keera's words. But instead, her silence left me spinning. What was she thinking? My head told me to run from someone who couldn't accept all of me. I'd been down that path, and it was a hard dead end. But my heart? My heart whispered that Jo was also a puzzle worth solving.

The only thing I knew for sure was the letters were real. Who knew where they would take the three of us eventually? Right now, they would keep me at Meerblick, the only place I wanted to be.

Leo had been right. Inside was an absolute treasure.

THE LETTERS

The Past: Eliza

December 28, 1925

Joelyn,

I write to you from Seattle. I don't know how to break the next part to you. I am married. To Henry.

It all happened in such a whirlwind. I am still reeling. Even now, sitting at this horrid desk at the Olympic Hotel, my hands trembling, I can scarcely believe it is true. One moment we were lying in front of the fire in my parents' house wrapped in each other's arms, as close as we could be, and now I am hundreds of miles away from you. After Father burst in on us, he dragged me out of the house. He threw clothes at me and shouted those foul words so loudly. Whore. Deviant. Disappointment. Did you hear them? All of the city must have heard them.

Joelyn, I want you to know that I fought to stay. I had thoughts of our running away together. But he shoved me back into the seat of the automobile. I attempted a lie to explain how he'd found us in such an unnatural manner. He was cold in his responses and told me how I was his only failure in life. Usually, he is all fire and brimstone in his anger, but there was something different about him, then and now, as if something in him broke. We broke it. I broke it. He wouldn't talk to me after that moment, not even to tell me where we were going.

As it turned out, it was Seattle. He had sent a telegram to Henry telling him to meet us at the hotel. Henry was all smiles and hugs when we got there, but something is different in him too.

Joelyn, God help me, they made a deal. Someone told Father about us. Who? I don't know. We were so careful, weren't we? In any case, Father agreed to support Henry's jazz career for two years, and if he hasn't made it after that time, he will set him up as a bigwig in Father's company. I understand why Father did it. He gets rid of me, the failure, the embarrassment, and maybe gets those grandsons he so obviously wants. But Henry? He sold out. He sold me out. He traded my happiness and future to make sure that he gets status and wealth. What is wrong with men? He knows that I don't love him and suspects that I love you. Father apparently never explicitly stated that part, but Henry has said a few things about you that make me think he knows too. That makes it so much worse. Suddenly, my friend is now another father, telling me that we will grow to love one another and other absolute nonsense. I will never forgive him.

I can hear you now saying, if I still feel like this, why did I marry him? If I am honest with myself, there are lots of reasons. Partly, I was a coward. I had Father, Henry, and this justice of the peace all glowering at me. All I had to do was say, "I do," to make some of that displeasure go away. I wasn't going to do it. I wanted to make a stand for you and for our love, but I made the mistake of looking into Father's eyes. Have you ever seen disappointment and disillusionment that goes all the way to the soul? Knowing those exact eyes would be on me for the rest of my life made me acquiesce.

Another reason is, in the back of my mind, I was thinking that I could have everything I wanted. If I satisfied them, I could later satisfy myself. At one point, I opened the door of our hotel room to find a phone to make a private call to you, but there was Robert, our own Robert, standing guard at the door. Has he been reading our letters all along? Did he give us away? I slammed the door in his face, the pig. Now I am reduced to sitting here in the middle of the night writing you a letter that I don't even know if I can post.

I must let you know two things. Father is personally putting us on a boat for South America tomorrow for our honeymoon. He has gotten over the fact that no self-respecting couple honeymoons anywhere but Europe. It was the only boat sailing tomorrow, and he told me that he will take no chances with me anymore. He also wants Henry to meet with some man there about growing fruit during our winter and their summer. He has visions of being the only store to sell bananas in January. Very romantic.

The second thing is that I will come back to you. I don't know how or even when. You must wait for me. When I get back, we will make that fairyland for ourselves. To hell with finding that fairy who grants wishes. We can do it ourselves.

I will contact you when I can. I know that I have no right to ask you for anything after what I have done. All I truly know is that I came alive that night at your house by the sea. It was the most important night and moment of my life. It was more than the two of us. The passion, the love, and the supreme tenderness gave the experience a life of its own, and the house holds our love. Go there, please, to think of me and my true wedding night.

I love you so very much. Wait for me!

E

P.S. I will never take my half of the Christmas heart off. Ever.

CHAPTER TEN

The Present: Hazel

"You're kidding me. That can't possibly be the end." Lauren slapped the sofa she was sitting on. "There has to be more."

We were back in the study that was quickly becoming our unofficial headquarters. The French doors stood open, hazy summer sunlight streamed in, and the gentle breeze brought the subtle, briny tang of the sea. None of it registered fully, though, because the second after Leo had left, we'd read the letters.

Well, Jo had. She lounged in an oversized chair, her legs draped casually over one arm. Reading out loud, she had started with Eliza's and Joelyn's tennis game and, without a break, carried us through to Eliza's declaration of love, pleading for Joelyn to wait.

Jo's reading voice was all liquid and soft at the edges. It slid through me like a gentle touch. There was something almost healing about it, smoothing over all the jagged cracks that Keera and her carousel of girlfriends had left.

Jo was also, surprisingly, a great actor. She gave Eliza a tender innocence that added to the drama of her story. Not that their love affair needed any more drama.

"That's it, Ren. Last one. There aren't any more." Jo turned the last letter over as if there might be a secret message scrawled on the back. It was crumpled in a way that suggested it had been read many times, maybe even thrown away, retrieved, and then carefully spread out. Jo handed it over, and I dropped it neatly on the pile that I'd been slowly building on the coffee table as she read them. Their love story in reverse.

On the sofa, Lauren brought her legs under her body. "Did Joelyn wait for her? Did they ever see each other again?"

"There's no way of knowing." Jo shrugged.

"Hazel, do you know? Are there any clues from the reflections?" Lauren wasn't giving up.

"Nothing beyond what I've already told you. We know that Clarissa knew about the letters. And that she and Jo were presumably fighting about them or the relationship in the past. We know that Joelyn's response was to hide them and her love away from everyone."

Lauren shook her head as if she wasn't buying it. "Clarissa seemed so forward thinking whenever she came up in Eliza's letters. I'm shocked she wouldn't support her daughter."

I sighed, the weight of the question settling over me. "Scandal is a lot easier to take when it doesn't hit close to home. Supporting a lesbian daughter in the 1920s is a lot harder than advocating for social justice at arm's length."

"We do know that Joelyn disappeared from the family record about this time." Count on Jo to bring everything back into focus.

"Maybe she ran away. To Europe. Paris, I hope." Lauren started to spin a story that was easy to get behind. "With Eliza. There, they could've lived on their own terms, away from judgment."

"Maybe," Jo said. "It would be nice to think so. But would she have left without this?"

She held up the only other item we'd found in the box, a breathtaking pendant: a black opal, vivid and otherworldly, set in eighteen karat gold and surrounded by diamonds. The pendant's design resembled a heart, purposely cut in half.

The Christmas heart.

It was far more extravagant and expensive than I'd imagined. And undeniably the kind of keepsake someone would take if they were running away with the love of their life.

"Probably not." Lauren pulled herself into an even tighter ball on the sofa. "She would've taken it."

"Especially if she gave the other half to Eliza." Jo carefully retied the faded ribbon around the letters I'd stacked, her hands steady. Her gaze was fixed on her task, pointedly avoiding mine. Why wouldn't she look at me? Something other than discovering the box had happened upstairs, but I had no idea what.

"Okay, so they probably didn't end up in Paris," Lauren said, oblivious, "but that doesn't mean it ended badly for them."

"I don't think we'll ever know."

Lauren sucked in a quick breath, almost a gasp. "We've talked about this. You can't lose faith, Jo. This isn't the end of their story or yours."

Yours? How was this the end of Jo's story?

Jo flinched, and her lips pinched tight. I'd been around her long enough to know it was her go-to move when annoyed.

Lauren turned to me. "Back me up here, Hazel."

What was she asking? I was stuck in the middle of a moment that was way heavier than it appeared on the surface. Jo had retreated behind walls that seemed less about shutting me out and more about protecting herself. Still, I desperately wanted in, to help her through whatever she was going through.

I rubbed the back of my neck, grappling with how to respond. I would answer a question that wasn't even on the table. "Everyone wants the recordings to answer the questions as if they're AI generated. They never do. The reflections were made long before the questions were even asked. Joelyn and Clarissa had no idea that we'd be sitting here now, piecing this all together. Sorry, this is the one thing I know. Whenever I see anything, the reflection brings up more questions than answers."

Jo slid a hand through her shiny hair, her expression still distant. Lauren shook her head. I wasn't surprised she didn't take "no" very well. "What? You're giving up too?"

"No. I'm saying that none of us can control what happens next. I mean, seeing Joelyn and Clarissa, finding the box, and hearing their story might be enough to quiet the energy in the house. Isn't that what you wanted?"

"Yes, but…"

"Look, I've seen this before," I added. "Reflections come and fade away like old photographs, and you lose the connection." What I didn't add was that the connection between me and Jo, this delicate bond we'd built over the last few days, was fading too. For me, that was what had made this adventure special. It was Lauren's first ride, but I'd been at this rodeo countless times.

"But could it also work the other way? We're part of the energy now. Maybe if you stay, you'll see more?"

Jo shook her head emphatically. "Ren, she has a life to get back to. We've already taken up too much of her time." Her tone wasn't harsh, just tired. Like she had been carrying something heavy for too long. The mysteries of the house? Camille? Me? Something else entirely?

Plain proof that people only got a fraction of the whole story, even when they were standing smack in the middle of it.

My stomach twisted into tight knots. My time at Meerblick was over. Was I acting like a petulant child? Maybe, but I didn't want to stay anywhere where I wasn't fully welcome. I got enough of that at my own gallery.

"Jo's right," I said finally. "I've got a couple of loose ends in my own life that I need to deal with." Keera and Cherry both loomed in front of me as if they were reflections. "Unfortunately," I said mostly to myself, "there's drama in the present too."

And just like that, the adventure was over. Way too abruptly, but that was how it was working out. I packed my things, promised Lauren I'd stay in touch, and almost said something to Jo when she handed me a travel mug of coffee. But I didn't.

Before I knew it, I stood on the gravel driveway next to my car. Edgar nosed my hand, and I crouched to give him a long hug. I rubbed my face in his soft fur. He was the one uncomplicated thing I was leaving behind. I wondered what I'd do with the pictures I'd taken of him.

Lauren wrapped me in her arms and squeezed tight. "I'm not letting this go," she whispered into my ear. "I'm going to talk to Jo."

Jo stood back, raising a hand in a silent farewell. There was no hug, no lingering glance, only a polite little wave. My stomach twisted again. I got in my car and drove down the driveway. The little pebbles crunched loudly under my tires.

Out on the highway, I called Lana, Keera's ex. "Any chance you can hold down the fort for one more day?" I asked, half expecting a hard no.

She didn't even hesitate. "Sure. I could use the cash." And then, almost as an afterthought, she said, "Oh, and you missed some big drama. Keera and Cherry had this massive blowout on the sidewalk outside the gallery. Something about New York. Keera told Cherry she wasn't going. I guess she had promised Cherry a trip there as part of the relationship package. She stormed off in one direction, Keera in the other. Man, if I hadn't been here, it would have been a real mess."

"Thank you," I said, genuinely grateful. I made a mental note to invite her out for drinks when all this chaos subsided. Maybe we could be friends?

Next, I called Gran. I needed the distraction.

She started in on me right away. Or at least, that was how I saw it. "You didn't give them much support. You shouldn't have left with those questions unanswered."

"I had nothing more to tell them. You know better than anyone that the gift gives when it wants and not when I ask."

"Forget the reflections. I'm not talking about their past. I'm talking about your future. Turn around and ask Jo what happened. It sounded like you were hitting it off."

I nearly choked. "Ha! I knew it. You were trying to set me up."

Silence spooled out of the car's speakers. I could picture her drumming her fingers on the dining room table, debating how much to admit.

"Maybe," she said eventually. "We didn't send you up for that reason, but we thought if you and Jo could get over yourselves, you might be a good match."

"Who's we?"

"Me, Jo's grandmother."

"And Lauren?"

"Yes, her too."

Unbelievable. "Look, Gran. It didn't work. I'm done begging women to explain their actions to me. I need someone open and honest from the get-go. Or imagine this, I need a relationship that doesn't even need explanations."

"Okay. Okay, I hear you, but sometimes, it's worth sticking around to see how the story unfolds—"

"Don't start, Gran," I cut her off. "You weren't wrong. I did like Jo. But I don't know who she is. And it doesn't look like I'm going to get a chance to."

"You could—"

"No, I couldn't." If I gave Gran any traction in this conversation, we'd soon be talking about what we'd name our kids all the way down the highway. "Do you want to hear about what was in the letters?"

She did, and with each detail, our exasperations melted away. She told me that I'd been a little emotional. I was supposed to read, rude. She wasn't wrong. Jo had gotten under my skin, and the fact that I was moving in the opposite direction, once again, from something I wanted was irritating. No excuse, though.

Like I said, the letters smoothed everything over. Even over the phone, I could feel Gran falling into the story.

When I got to the part about Eliza's visit to Meerblick, I said, "And then they finally consummated their relationship."

"About time," Gran replied.

We rolled right into Eliza running from her feelings as fast as she could. And then her marriage. I didn't do Eliza justice. The story spilling from the silver box was obviously her personal interpretation. She had been telling Joelyn what had happened, and she had been there for most of it. But Eliza had used the letters to process the events too. They were filtered, reconstructed, infused with personal intention. That was what I could appreciate about the reflections. They often felt like the unvarnished truth. No ego, no agenda. Life as it happened.

But here was the rub: I wasn't an observer in this story. I'd *participated.*

Sitting in the den, listening to Jo read, I hadn't only imagined Eliza and Joelyn's first kiss. I'd experienced it. Eliza leaning in bit by bit, hesitation giving way to the weight of longing. Joelyn standing stock still, heart pounding out of her chest, terrified that even the tiniest movement would scare Eliza off. Their lips finally touching, at first barely brushing and then grabbing what they had wanted for months. As I'd sat there listening to Jo, sensual flutters had spun low in my stomach.

So whose story was it? Theirs? Jo's? Mine? Maybe all of ours?

And the dream? I didn't tell Gran about *that.* Hell, I was barely letting myself think about it. But I too had seen Joelyn in that sheer nightgown. I'd seen the erotic curve of her breasts, a stomach that begged to be caressed, and how had Eliza called it? *Lower shadows* that promised all sorts of pleasures. Lips and fingers and shivers had come at me from all directions, and even now, the ache from that experience was so close.

Their passion simmered inside me. It was still there when I got into bed that night. The memories washed over me, and for a heartbeat, I hoped I could fall back into the fantasy.

Nothing came. I slept through the night, dreamless and untouched. Instead, I woke up to wild pounding on my front door. Bolting upright, I flew through my condo. Peering through my peephole, I saw, of all people, Cherry.

Legs planted wide, fists curled into balls, she stood large in the fish-eye distortion. She was dressed in skintight yoga pants and a matching bra, and she glared right at the peephole as if she knew I was watching.

"Hazel," she cried, "I know you're in there."

How? I'd been home for just over twelve hours. Was she stalking my condo now?

"Open the door."

Sighing deeply, I did but stepped into the doorway so she couldn't rush in.

"What could you possibly want?" I asked, trying to keep my voice even.

"I want to know why you're out to get me. Why'd you make Keera break up with me?"

"What?" All my muscles went rigid. "I didn't—"

"Yes, you fucking did." She was practically snarling. "We fought yesterday at the gallery, and she invited me over last night. I thought it was to apologize. But she told me that you were right. I wasn't working out. She said you told her that."

I bit my lip. I could remember the exact moment in the gallery when I had said that. But in no universe was this on me. Keera had wanted the breakup.

"And then she threw in extra shade. That I wasn't working out anywhere. Not in the gallery or in the bedroom." Cherry's voice cracked, and tears welled up in her eyes.

Ouch. I could hear Keera saying that. She had always been one to weaponize sex.

"She told me that she needed to move in a new direction with her life. And that I wasn't part of it."

"Oh my God," I said under my breath. Keera had never taken my advice before. "I'm so sorry, Cherry."

And I was. I'd been on the breakup end of that same conversation with Keera. It wasn't fun.

Cherry swayed slightly, her anger giving way to despair. "I'd already told my roommate I was leaving. I thought I was going over there to grab the key and start moving in."

That was kind of what I'd thought too. Or at least before Lana had told me about their sidewalk scuffle.

"Then, outta nowhere, she hits me with, like, that's not happening, and right after that, she's like, we're done." Her voice cracked again. "I mean, what am I supposed to do now? Shanda already has some rando moving in to take my spot." A tear slipped down her cheek. "I really thought she was the one, you know?"

Dammit. Cherry was beyond self-centered, and impossibly

young, but heartbreak looked the same on anyone. I knew exactly how she felt.

That was how Cherry ended up curled on my sofa hugging a throw pillow to her chest.

She talked. I listened. She spilled everything, starting with how Keera had found her in a bar one night. Even told me Keera's pickup line. "I'm bored, and you look like a lovely diversion." That was pretty much the exact pitch she had used with me, although I hadn't gotten the lovely part. Cherry even described their first night together in excruciating detail. She had gone down on Keera three times. She started to tell me how Keera liked her oral sex: lots of aggressive sucking with gentle little flicks of the tongue. I held up my hand for her to stop.

"I don't need the specifics." Besides, I already knew.

Keera had apparently made lots of promises. That sounded familiar as well. For Cherry, that had included a modeling contract that had never materialized, a trip to New York, and a fantastic job at the gallery.

"No hate. The job at the gallery sucks." She glanced at me, but there was no real apology in her look. "Just saying."

"I get it." I let her off the hook. We both knew she didn't belong at the gallery.

"I stayed because Keera had me down bad, like, she really got in my head. She had me thinking that I was nobody without her. For real."

I got that too.

"You need to talk to her. Tell her to take me back. We're good together."

"Oh, Cherry," I said as gently as I could. "She doesn't listen to me. She only listens to herself."

Honestly, that could've described Cherry too, but she still had twenty years to grow up and maybe become a different person.

I needed to wrap this up and get her to the door. Not that I needed a reminder, but Cherry's experience with Keera was a serious wake-up call. I didn't need to make this all about me, but I had to get a lawyer ASAP.

Cherry tucked her feet underneath her legs. She had her tennis shoes on, but that didn't stop her. She took a deep breath and ran through the whole sad story again. This time, I let her vent, and when she finally finished, she hugged the pillow and raised her eyebrows in desperation. "You gotta help me."

"I'll make a few job calls on your behalf," I said as I led her to the door.

She planned to crash on Shanda's couch—not rent free, she told me—while she waited for everyone else, including me, to solve her problems. At least the tears had dried up by the time she stepped outside.

"Take good care," I said as I closed the door and let out a long, exhausted breath.

That left me thinking about Keera. What an asshole. She had taken out all her frustration with me on poor Cherry. Not that I was Team Cherry now, but I didn't wish her ill. And like I'd said, I had stood in her shoes. Not comfortable.

The bigger issue was Keera herself. Unmoored, unpredictable, and I was sure practically vibrating with the chaos she had created. I was ashamed to say that while Cherry was knee-deep in her problems for the second time, I'd quietly started formulating a plan.

I walked to my kitchen and slid out my junk drawer. Inside, the usual mess greeted me: random cords to devices I didn't even own anymore, more than a few stray nuts and bolts, and a stack of business cards secured with a binder clip. Sometimes, when I was on location, celebrity managers would slip me a card on the sly, telling me to hang on to it in case I needed new representation one day. I wasn't quite there yet, but they didn't know that, and I did need their advice.

I cold-called the ones I remembered as not total jerks and asked if they knew any good lawyers. A bunch didn't answer, or their assistants wouldn't connect me. But three did recommend the same lawyer right here in the city. She was my next call.

Unbelievably, Marianne Kenning was available, and after signing a digital retainer, I sent her a copy of the contract.

"Your partner knows what she's doing," she said when she called me back. "The contract is very tight. Is she reasonable?"

"No."

She chuckled lightly, but her tone remained professional. "Do you want a revised contract with new terms, or do you want to terminate?"

I had to think about that for a beat. Could Keera and I still work together if we were truly equal partners in the business? After all, our bottom line for many years had been very successful. But success had come at a cost. My self-worth, my creativity, my voice. Could Keera ever truly change? Did I want to risk that?

"I don't know," I said uselessly. I couldn't even walk through a door when it was opened for me. My indecision felt like its own failure.

"You have several options." She quickly spun into legalese. "Although, I must advise you, each option is likely to incur significant costs. I can approach Keera to discuss the possibility of modifying the existing contract to better align with your requirements. Alternatively, you could propose a buyout. Pay her to step away. That route often avoids litigation."

She took a breath before her next rapid-fire burst. "Another option would be to initiate a legal claim for breach of contract. However, this path can trigger countersuits and escalate quickly with mounting legal fees. Sometimes, the prospect of extensive legal fees and court proceedings serves as a deterrent, encouraging parties to pursue an amicable resolution instead."

My mind swam.

"It's a lot to think about," she said, echoing my thoughts.

"No kidding."

"This isn't just business, is it?"

"No."

"Consider your options, and get back to me. I'm here to advise you further."

I didn't need more time. I needed to get the ball rolling, take back control. "Reach out to her. I want to control my own bookings and sign off on how and where my photos can be used. Oh, and can we add something that says if she violates the contract, it's terminated?"

"We can absolutely draft something to protect your interests."

All I wanted was my power back. "Thank you."

"I'll make contact. It's unlikely that she'll engage directly, though. If she's as prudent as she seems, we'll be dealing with her attorney. But we can start without delay."

Hope spooled through my chest as I hung up. Keera was going to hate this, but if she wanted to continue our partnership, she was going to have to roll with the punches. She'd be the one to adapt.

Me too, for that matter. I grabbed my computer and scrolled through the Instagrams of some of the live animal mascots in college football. For months, I'd been sitting on this idea and hadn't worked up the nerve to pitch it. Keera had been chipping away at my self-worth much longer than she had been giving Cherry grief.

My screen lit up with a lineup of majestic creatures: a gorgeous white falcon, gleaming white horses, a huge Russian boar, and a cast of dogs, Alaskan malamutes, collies, coonhounds, bulldogs. There were so many to choose from, and not a single pop star in sight.

Sure, creating a calendar, posters, or publicity shots for these mascots would come with a host of contractual headaches, but this project had real potential. Keera could prove her worth by locking down copyrights, royalties, and licensing fees. Once a few universities and colleges signed on, the rest would clamor to be part of it. And me? I could road trip across the country taking pictures of these incredible animals.

Even better, I could layer in a greater purpose, partnering with an organization for animal conservation. What school wouldn't want to look good while helping animals?

With Lana taking care of business at the gallery, I'd have a full day to dive in. Pulling a notebook from a bookshelf, I started sketching out the idea. Each school, its mascot, their visual style. The details quickly took shape. I was so wrapped up in the idea that the whole morning and most of the afternoon flew by. When I finally dropped my mechanical pencil onto the table, the sun had dipped toward the Golden Gate Bridge.

My stomach let out an embarrassing growl, reminding me I hadn't eaten since…yesterday? Sadly, there was no French-inspired chef with a lovely voice standing in my kitchen, eager to whip up a delicious meal for two. Takeout it was.

An hour later, night had crept into the neighborhood. I walked back from my favorite Chinese restaurant, clutching my usual order of hot and sour soup and chicken fried rice. I was always a little ashamed that I never ventured further down the menu to something more adventurous, but D-Lee Great Eastern classics never disappointed.

The plan for the night was simple: dump the rice and soup into my favorite blue bowl, curl up on the couch, and stream the new lesbian rom-com everyone had been raving about. If I could shove the Jo, Eliza, and Joelyn drama out of my head, it'd be the perfect evening.

THE JOURNAL

The Past: Joelyn

At last.

You are in my arms. Do you know how long I have waited for this? My hands are on the back of your neck. Running my fingers through your hair. Your hair, so short now. It tickles my palms. I could spend all day pulling my fingers through it. The way my touch makes you arch your neck. Looking up at me. Eyes blue, golden, sparkling in a million colors at once. Open so wide. In what. Surprise? Concern? Desire? I lean down to kiss each one. They shut and stay shut as a small moan escapes your lips. You feel it too. It is the first time my lips have touched you anywhere except for that kiss, that morning kiss. What is this I feel? Longing, for sure. But something else as well. As if this connection is bigger than we are. It feels so right. Yes. I knew it would be like this. You move into me, yielding. We are so close now, I can smell the day on you. The beach, the lavender you always wear, the smell of sunshine on your skin. I drink it in as I cup your face in my hands. And then I stop to look at you. Really look. I want to remember this moment always. Have it burned into my mind long after this day and our time is gone. Is that possible?

We lean into each other, and finally, after all these months, our lips meet. Soft, full, tender. Your mouth gives way at once; it moves under mine. Your lips part slightly. I can feel the wonder of this moment passing from you to me through the kiss. All these months of waiting are finally over. This is all I have ever wanted.

At last.

CHAPTER ELEVEN

The Present: Hazel

As I rounded the corner to my condo, a blur of boundless energy and black and white fur barreled toward me. Edgar. His leash dangled behind him as he sprinted full tilt. He launched himself at me, paws at my waist, nudging me with his head.

"Edgar!"

My pulse spiked, an unexpected thrill buzzing through me. Because behind him, there Jo was. Trotting down the street, waving her arms at her defiant dog. Gracefully, fluidly moving through the space between us. I couldn't believe how much I'd missed watching her. It had only been one day.

"Edgar," She grabbed the leash and pulled him gently off me. "Sorry about that."

"Don't worry. I'll take it as a compliment." I smiled, happy to see her.

She laughed, a little sheepish. "He really likes you."

"I really like him," I said, hoping she'd get the hint that *him* included her too. "What brings you here? Not that I'm complaining. But I'm a little surprised."

"Honestly, I am too. I don't usually do impulsive things like this."

My smile widened, hoping her spontaneity was a good sign. "I live up there." I nodded to a door down the block. We started walking, falling easily into step.

"Lauren practically pushed me out the door. We talked a lot last night after you left, and we might have had one too many apple brandies. Eventually, she let slip that she and our grandmother had this whole big plan. Sure, they were interested in the history of the house, but they were also hoping that it would bring us together." She laid a hand over her breastbone. "I'm so sorry."

I stopped, letting the words sink in. "Don't be. My Gran was scheming too. Everyone was in on it. So let me get this straight. You came all the way down here to say you're sorry?" I had to admit, I was disappointed.

"Yeah, and..." She rolled her head around as if she was unsure she wanted to continue.

"And?"

"And...to explain what happened yesterday. Why I turned off."

I turned toward her, hugging my food to my chest. This, I wanted to hear.

"Okay, I can't believe I'm saying this practically in the middle of the street," she began, "but I was in a relationship back in France. I was in love. Then one day, I walked into our flat and found her with... someone else." She made a small popping noise with her lips like she still couldn't believe it.

Without thinking, I reached out, sliding my hand down her arm. She tensed up, but I let my fingers linger. "I'm so sorry."

"Thanks." She took a slight step back, and I let my hand fall. "I've had time to process, but it still stings when I think about it. Which is way more than I should. That kind of hurt, it doesn't go away. And it's made me cautious, maybe too cautious with other people."

God, I knew exactly how she felt. Edgar, also picking up on her tension, whined softly.

Jo reached down and ruffled his fur and, with her gaze fixed downward, kept talking, "So here's the deal. When we were in the Blue Room, tearing into the wall and finding nothing but dust, I was mad. Furious, really. At you because I thought you had never seen anything, and now you were lying to us while we were destroying our house. And at myself, mostly myself, because you had gotten to me. Before Leo came over, I was beginning to believe."

I voiced my hurt. "But we found the box."

"I know." She finally looked up, and I caught the flash of pain in her eyes. "That made everything worse. I should've trusted my gut and had faith in you all along. I should've known that one betrayal doesn't mean everyone's like that." Her fears probably tugged at her, and her gaze slipped away from mine.

"What made me the maddest, though, was the awful part of me thought that maybe I didn't deserve a shot with you. Like somehow, I'd brought all that mess with Camille onto myself." She toyed with the neckline of her sweater. "I'm scared, Hazel. Really scared."

She stepped back in, setting my bag of takeout on the ground between us. "Edgar, sit." The dog obeyed instantly. Her hands found mine, her fingers surprisingly steady against my trembling ones. "The thing is, Lauren made me realize something. You make me want to be brave. And God, that's scarier than anything else."

Her words struck me. My heart wasn't just racing. It was dancing, soaring, reaching for something I'd spent a long time waiting for. I didn't know it would be Jo, and I didn't know it would be now. But this feeling, alive and safe, wrapped up in possibility? All I had to do was reach out and claim it.

"I get it. You've no idea how much I get it," I said softly, my voice thick with the weight of all the things I'd tell her later. "But here's another thing. The most important thing. You don't have to be brave at all. We can be scared together." I squeezed her hands gently. "We barely know each other. I, for one, would love to see where this could go. And if you, or I, need to take a step back sometimes, that would be okay, right? I don't want to step away completely before we even try."

Fuck. Had I said that? There was no going back now. My heart hammered against my ribs as I waited for her answer.

"Me neither." A smile lit up her face as she offered me her arm. I scooped up the food and linked my arm through hers, savoring how perfectly we fit together. We started to my door in a silence that hummed with possibility.

When we arrived, she tilted her head back, studying my building. "Nice."

"And brand-new. There're no reflections in my condo. No one's lived there but me. That's the best part."

"Oh, is that how it works?"

"I have no idea." A laugh bubbled up, and she grinned. Was this what easy banter with Jo would feel like?

I lifted the bag of takeout. "Do you want to come up? It's just soup and rice, but there's enough for two."

She nodded and closed the space between us. So close I could feel her warm breath on my cheek. "Can I do something first? What I should have done that night in Clarissa's room." Her eyes dropped to my lips and then back up.

My turn to nod, unable to find the words to say yes. Her nearness was intoxicating, and my pulse spiked in anticipation of what would come next. I wanted this more than I could say.

She reached up to tuck a wayward curl behind my ear, and her fingers lingered, tracing first the curve of my ear and dropping to the edge of my jaw. Her touch left trails of desire in their wake. Her other hand found my waist and tugged me closer until our foreheads almost touched. On my hip, her hand trembled slightly, and I heard the tiny catch in her breath that betrayed her nervousness.

Edgar chose that moment to let out a contented groan and nestle between our feet. We chuckled, and thanks to him, all first-kiss jitters melted into the night.

We both leaned in, the space between us shrinking heartbeat by heartbeat. My eyes fluttered closed, anticipating that first, electric brush of her lips. This was it. The start of something wonderful.

"What the fuck? Are you kissing my partner?" A sharp voice sliced through the air.

The sharp clack of heels echoed down the sidewalk. We both spun to the sound.

It was Keera.

She eyed us with a look that could have frozen fire. "I come all this way to take you to New York, and I find…this?" Her tone was cold, lethal. Jo staggered back like she had taken a physical hit.

"Business partner," I sputtered. "Just business." I tried to grab Jo's hand to pull her back to my side, but she shook me off. She wouldn't even look at me. My perfect night was unraveling faster than I could put it back together.

Keera waved airline tickets in front of us as if they were a real weapon. "We can leave tonight."

Did they even print tickets anymore except at the airport? Had she known Jo was here? What the hell? I took a step toward Jo, and Edgar jumped in between us. He didn't growl, but the message was clear. He was standing guard. Against me, dammit. "Let me explain."

Jo held up her palm, stopping me cold. "No. Don't bother. I don't even want to know what is going on here." With her chin high, she headed to a parked car, Edgar trotting behind her. "I can't believe I let Lauren talk me into doing this. I must have been out of my mind to jump into another bad situation."

"Jo, wait," I called after her, but my words fell flat.

She didn't pause or turn. Within seconds, she leapt in her car and sped off. The red taillights faded down the street, mocking me the whole way.

I whirled back to Keera, anger boiling over. She flashed her most dazzling smile and once again waved the tickets in the air. This time like a prize. I wasn't biting. "What the fuck, Keera?"

"I'd thought I surprise you." Her voice dripped with fake hurt. "Who doesn't love first class?"

"That's not what I mean, and you know it." I glared at her, tall and elegant in her cashmere sweater and two hundred dollar jeans. Then it hit me. I didn't have to play her game anymore. It took two to play, and I, much to my happy surprise, had finally heard the game over whistle. At least Jo had left me that. "I've hired a lawyer. You should too. I want out, and I'll do whatever it takes to end this partnership."

The last three words flew out with a venom I didn't know I had. Juggling the takeout bag, I punched the keypad code with more force than necessary. I needed to get away from her as fast as possible.

The door clicked open, and before I could step inside, Keera grabbed my arm, spinning me around to face her. The door clicked behind me, locking us into a moment that was the exact inverse of me and Jo.

Her eyes locked on mine. "I want you back."

My stomach twisted, tightening into a hard knot. "You didn't hear me. We're not going to be in business together anymore."

She shrugged, her expression unreadable. "Forget the business. We'll sort it out or not. I'm talking about us. As a couple." She took a measured breath, a bit too slow, like she was calculating her next move. "It took seeing you in the arms of another woman to realize it." She smirked like she was proud of this sudden awareness. "I broke up with Cherry, you know."

I stared, too stunned to respond. She seemed to take my silence as a win, and like a coiled snake, she moved in for the kill. Without asking, she kissed me hard, and to my horror, I remembered the fantasies I'd had all the way up the coast. All of them had ended like this. Keera appearing out of nowhere, begging for another chance and crushing her mouth against mine. The sweetness. The surrender. I had wanted it so badly.

Not anymore. In fact, I was repulsed. This wasn't love or passion. It was control. I shoved her away with my free hand, pushing into her chest with a force that surprised us both.

"Stop," I said, my voice thankfully steady. "I don't want this—or you—anymore."

She tried to brush it off, waving her hand dismissively. "Hazel, consider the big picture. We could have it all. The perfect relationship and the perfect business partnership."

I let out a short, sharp laugh. "We already tried that, remember? I wasn't enough for you then, and it's not going to be enough for me now. Excuse me. I have dinner waiting."

Her whole body stiffened, and she jabbed the air with a sharp finger. "This is a huge mistake. You're not going to get these big contracts without me."

There it was. The seduction and the supposed epiphany had only ever been about business. Not that I hadn't known, but this was the first time I had ever allowed myself to see her for the master manipulator that she was.

"Probably not, but that's a risk I'm willing to take," I said, almost relishing the annoyed look that flitted across her face. "Especially since I know for sure *you'll* never get those contracts without me. Who else can do what I do?" I keyed in the code again, and this time, when the door clicked open, I slipped through before she could react. "I finally realize I have all the power here," I said over my shoulder as the door swung shut.

Don't turn around, I told myself. I wanted to. I wanted to see if I'd hit my mark and if my words had left any impact.

The elevator door slid open, and I stepped in, head down. I didn't check. I had my priorities all wrong. Keera didn't matter anymore, not one little bit. My only concern now was figuring out how I was going to get Jo back.

I texted Lauren for help on the way up in the elevator and again while my soup spun in the microwave, then before I brushed my teeth, and finally after I flicked off the bedroom light. Each message laid out a little more of the story. She didn't answer a single one. For someone who liked to be involved, it seemed odd. Had Jo gotten to her first? If she had already heard Jo's version of our night, maybe she thought I was no better than Camille.

I needed to break it all down with Gran. I called and gave her the play-by-play, starting with Cherry and every other detail until I got to Keera. Finally, I reached the real reason I'd called. "Can you call their grandmother and find out what Jo's thinking? You're already involved, and Lauren's ghosting me, no pun intended."

"When did you go back to middle school?"

"If you want me to drop this, I will," I lied. "But you started it, and I'm admitting you were right."

"Sorry. I didn't catch that. Could you say that again?" She was having way too much fun at my expense.

"Fine. You were right. Jo and I could be a good match. I don't have her number. And since Lauren's gone radio silent, I've no way to get in touch with her."

"Yes, sweetheart. I'll hang up and call Jeannie right now. I love you. Especially since you said I was right."

The next morning, still no call or text. I showered and threw on jeans and a baggy sweatshirt that had *DOPE Photographer* printed boldly across the front. It had been a gag gift from a college friend, and with laundry piling up, I had zero choices. Later, I wished I'd dug deeper into my closet and put more thought into my outfit, but I'll get to that.

I stopped at Brewed Bliss for a latte, happy for the warmth seeping through the cup, and headed straight to the gallery. I didn't know what I expected, maybe to see it in ruins after my days of neglect, but it stood tall and strong with *Hazel Ross Gallery* etched into the stone lintel above the door. My talent had built this place, and I couldn't let Keera forget that.

Inside, the big industrial space echoed around me. No Cherry in sight, thankfully, and unsurprisingly, no Keera either. It was just me and my photographs. I couldn't remember the last time I'd stood here alone, soaking it in.

Front and center was a big print of a GloFish, a genetically engineered glow-in-the-dark zebrafish. Neon green, it peered freakishly from its huge aquarium, and even I had to admit, greeted viewers with a bang as soon as they walked in the door.

This print was the highlight of my last celebrity shoot with singer superstar Suki Lush. Keera and I had flown to Las Vegas where Suki had a residency and had spent a hellish two days with her three boys, all under five, their nannies, one vet, and more pets than I could count. Each boy had his own exotic menagerie, including a bearded dragon, a Bengal cat, a hedgehog, a pygmy pig, and Kepper the GloFish. Suki Lush had asked for "pocket size" photographs so that the boys, as she delightedly told us, could keep their animals in their pockets. She wanted them to be able to pull the pictures out whenever they were lonely.

They were surrounded by so many people and animals that I didn't see how this was even possible, but I had to give it to Keera: the prints that came out of those two days made for an excellent show. Besides the animals, Suki Lush was in enough behind-the-scenes candids to bring in her fans, and despite Cherry's incompetence, the gallery had done well selling postcards or calendars, a pack of notecards, or full prints of less famous and more fortunate animals. Keera had called it her best bait and switch. I was proud of what I'd done for Suki Lush, but I was also thinking of a different type of show.

The door behind me chimed, and I turned to see Lana stride in. Her pastel leather slides tapped against the floor, and her highlighted hair shimmered in the gallery lights. Everything about her screamed Keera's type, except for the sharp intelligence in her eyes. I stood awkwardly for a moment, not knowing how to greet her, but hell, this was a new me. I pulled her into a quick, friendly hug.

"You've been a lifesaver these last few days," I said, letting go, hoping that she could see how much I meant it.

"Happy to help." And then, she said a little sheepishly, "Actually came by to see if you needed one more day? I'm going to be honest. I'm in a bit of a bind, and another shift would help."

An idea sparked. "What would you think about something a little more permanent?"

"Seriously? I'd love that." She met my gaze with a frank openness that hadn't been in this gallery for ages. "I need to be clear. I still want to focus on creating content."

I loved that she was up-front with her needs. "We could work around that. Create a schedule that works for both of us. And as you know, the gallery doesn't officially open until eleven. That would leave you the morning?"

Lana nodded and then hesitated. "Does Keera have a say in this? She wasn't exactly thrilled when I showed up the other day."

"I imagine not." I was embarrassed when I smirked. "Let's say the gallery is restructuring. Keera won't be making the front-of-house hires anymore."

"About time." She threw out a fist bump. "Good for you, Hazel."

I returned the bump. I took a deep breath, and my tone turned serious. "I need to ask. You don't have designs on Keera in any way? To let you know, I'm taking all inappropriate romance out of this workplace."

Lana's laugh, bright and honest, rang through the gallery. "Please. I saw through her pretty quickly."

"Right." I wish I could have said the same, but better late than never. "I'm going into the back. Call me if you need anything."

"Go. I've got this."

I walked away with a new lightness in my step. Moving on felt pretty damn good. This wasn't about ending the partnership or reclaiming the gallery. It was about rediscovering who I was. And finally putting myself first.

THE JOURNAL

The Past: Joelyn

Our Touch

Burning into me. I am lost as you yield your body to mine. Our kiss deepens until I can feel it resonating throughout my whole being. We break, breathless, and I run a trail of kisses from the corner of your mouth to your neck. So slender and smooth. I take a moment to breathe your smell in again and then slide my lips down your chest until I can feel your heart beating wildly under them. I nestle my head there and listen to the rhythm for a minute, and then, slowly, I move over. I can feel your chest rising and falling under the sheer fabric of your nightgown. I brush my face, my lips, across your breasts, slowly at first, faster as I feel you respond. Then, as I hear you moan, I move back up to your mouth. Crushing it under mine. Together, we create a pulsing energy that spreads out to fill the room. It lingers and circles back to almost embrace us. This moment is more than our first night together. I know that it binds us for all time. Here and now and for always. It is your touch. It is my touch.

Our touch.

CHAPTER TWELVE

The Present: Hazel

Edgar, in different poses and guises, stared at me from my monitors in my workspace. I ran a hand through my tangled hair and let out a long breath. These photos were something else. My photos had been flat and emotionless for months, and these were electric, alive. My pulse quickened. Maybe I had my mojo back.

Maybe it was just the Jo part.

The printer hummed to life as I queued up the best shots. The prints wouldn't have that professional lab polish, but this wasn't about gallery perfection. This was about watching Jo's face when she saw them. The real question was, how did I get them, her, and me all in the same room?

I stared at my phone. Lauren's name sat on top like a challenge. My unanswered messages lined the screen like desperate little blue flags, waving without one response. If I sent even one more, I'd officially become a stalker.

I pinched and tugged at my bottom lip. Was there another plan? And then, almost as if I had summoned her from a void, three dots popped up. Lauren was typing.

I'm coming to get you. Where are you?

I sent her the gallery address without hesitation.

Be there in twenty minutes.

And then, naturally, I spent the next twenty minutes pacing and overthinking. I was out on the curb early, waiting when a metallic orange Mustang SUV came screaming down the street. It slammed on its brakes and rolled down its window.

"Get in. We're late." Lauren sat in the driver's seat, chin jutting out. She was on a mission.

I was still fumbling with my seat belt when she floored the car out into rushing traffic.

"Late for what? Where are we going?" My knuckles went white on the door handle.

"I found her." She threw both hands up into the air in triumph, and the car swerved wildly on the road.

"Jo?"

"No. Eliza." She paused for dramatic effect. "Well, her relatives. Parked myself in the den with my laptop, no phone, no distractions, and didn't stop until I found them."

I guess that explained the ghosting. She launched into a blow-by-blow account of her methods that would have impressed me if I hadn't seen my life expectancy dropping by the mile. She sped up before she took a turn, and her braking at stop signs was like skidding to avoid hitting a runaway baby carriage. I clung to my seat and prayed that this fancy Mustang had top-tier airbags.

"They live here!" With a grand flourish, her hands once again flew off the wheel. "Still in Pacific Heights. At the same freaking house as Eliza's letters. Can you believe our luck? I found Durham House. It still exists."

She smacked the steering wheel in joy. The car swerved again, and I fought down my impulse to grab the wheel.

She jolted to a stop, and I stared up at architectural royalty. A freestanding house right in the middle of the city. It was breathtakingly gorgeous, fully restored in clean, simple lines. A long stairway flanked by stone lions led to the wood and glass front door.

"Eliza lived here?"

Lauren laughed, not unkindly. "No, this is Nob Hill. I thought you grew up here?"

"I did. I'm just…" How could I explain that after that ride, I could barely see straight, all turned around.

"This is my house. Technically, my parents'." She tilted her head and spoke into her phone. "I'm here. Time to move. We're late."

My heart did a stupid, little skip. I knew better than to hope.

"This is the other house that Claude built during his lifetime. Before Meerblick. It's way too big for the three of us, but my family likes to hang on to things. It has—oh, my God, Hazel. I bet you'd see a million reflections here. Promise me when this is all over, you'll come back and look."

I never liked to seek out reflections. As usual, however, she didn't wait for an answer.

"Everyone could be here. I'd love for you to meet my five-greats grandfather. God, I'd give anything to know what he got up to behind closed doors."

Dangerous territory. Some stones, I'd learned, were better left unturned. The idea, however, had seized her. When she pushed for a real answer, I nodded. "Sure."

The front door opened, and Jo appeared, moving down the stairs like gravity was optional for her. She had that fresh from the shower look and wore her jeans and sweater like haute couture. My mouth went dry.

She, on the other hand, almost recoiled when she saw me sitting in the front seat. Something flickered over her face, too quick for me to read, gone before I could even try. "Hazel?" My name came out careful and measured, not exactly cold but guarded. "What are you doing here?"

I forced a weak laugh. "Honestly, no clue. I think I'm being kidnapped."

She didn't smile as I'd hoped and only said, "Lauren does have that effect on people."

"Ah, geez, Jo. I told them we'd all be there ten minutes ago. You know how I hate to be late."

Jo planted her feet on the sidewalk. Lauren rolled her eyes. "For God's sake, get in the car. We have a chance to find out what happened to Eliza and Joelyn. We owe it to them." She looked from Jo to me. "We owe it to ourselves. We started this together. We need to finish that way too."

"Fine," Jo said finally. "But I'm driving."

"I can drive. I'm already sitting here."

"Yes, but I want to get there alive." Jo walked around the driver's side and opened the door. For all her bravado earlier, Lauren slid out meekly and got into the back seat.

We drove in awkward silence made even worse by the silence of the car. It was electric. Lauren eventually leaned forward. "You're going to be civil when we get there, Jo, aren't you? I don't know exactly what happened last night, and I never got your side of the story. I just—"

"Leave it, Lauren," Jo said curtly.

"I think—"

"Please," Jo pleaded. Her voice was strained. "Leave it."

Lauren fidgeted in the back seat, opening her mouth a few times but saying nothing. As the car doled out the directions, I stared out the passenger window. Jo's presence, two feet away, threw me into a tizzy. I couldn't relax. I hated, actually loathed, not knowing where we stood.

"There it is." Lauren pointed to another stately house on a corner as the car announced our arrival. "Oh, and there's a parking space. See, fate has our backs."

"Really, Ren?" Jo expertly parallel-parked in a space barely bigger than the car.

Lauren bounded out, already halfway up the path before Jo had even turned off the engine. She left me and Jo to walk up to the house together alone.

"Nice sweatshirt." Her tone was unreadable.

I looked down to remember that I was wearing the *DOPE Photographer* hoodie. Heat flushed my cheeks, and I didn't know why, but I said, "Thanks. I am."

Ahead, Lauren chatted into the intercom, and the door buzzed open, revealing a lovely foyer.

"It's condos now. They're on the second floor," Lauren announced.

"Who's they?" Jo asked.

I shrugged in response. We followed Lauren to a door marked with an elaborate, curling number 2. She knocked firmly, and a woman in her late thirties opened the door. She was blond and pretty, glowing in that "I never miss a Pilates class" kind of way. An excited grin lit up her face as soon as she saw us. She looked a lot like Eliza on the beach over one hundred years ago.

"Oh my God. Are you Lauren?" Her eyes darted to Jo because, of course, who wouldn't look at Jo first?

"No, I am," Lauren said, unflinching as always. She never shrank in Jo's shadow. Her confidence was growing on me, not that I'd ever let her drive me one short block ever again.

"Thanks for agreeing to see us," Lauren added, stepping forward. "I know this is random coming out of the blue. But I swear, we're for real. No scams. I promise."

"That's okay. I have the police on speed dial." She laughed and stuck out her hand with no hesitation. "Nice to meet you. I'm Lynn."

"Hear that, Jo? Her name is Lynn. Jo, meet Lynn. Together, you're Joelyn."

"Not a coincidence, I gather." Jo shook her counterpart's hand,

and her shoulders dropped, relaxing a little into whatever this was. "And this is our friend, Hazel," Jo added without looking at me.

Lynn's excitement spilled over as she stepped back, ushering us inside. "I can't believe you're here. Come in. Come in." The apartment was large, airy, and modern. She gestured to another blond woman by the sofa, her grin as infectious. "This is my sister, Maggie. You couldn't know this, but you're hopefully the answer to a family mystery that we have wondered about since we were kids."

Lauren clapped her hands. "This gets better and better." She plopped into a wingback chair, eager for whatever was coming next.

"Joelyn is a family name for us too," Lynn said as she brought tea, iced and hot, from the kitchen on a tray. We'd settled in the living room. "My great grandmother was named Joelyn in honor of a friend of her mother's, and I was named for her."

"And I was named for our mother, Margaret. Our family has a limited pool of names." Maggie laughed.

There was something so genuine about them both. They had an effortless ease that dissolved the tension from the car ride. For the first time since Lauren had scooped me up, we were all exactly where we were supposed to be. Sitting in this living room, sipping tea, and participating in something much larger than ourselves.

Lauren leaned in, and her voice dropped to a conspiratorial whisper. "Well," she said, "Jo was named after your great-great grandmother's friend. She's the original Joelyn. Our great-great-great aunt." She pulled the beach photograph seemingly from thin air like a magic trick. She pointed to it. "That's Joelyn. That's Eliza. The rest are our family. Jo and I come from Lewis, here." She slid her finger to the goofy boy on the edge of the frame.

Maggie bent closer, squinting at the image. "Lynn, look at her. She's so young."

"I didn't even realize she knew the Stewards. Your family's practically San Francisco royalty." Lynn cleared her throat in embarrassment. "I mean, I didn't even know they were friends."

Lauren, never one to bury the lede, smiled slyly. "They were more than friends. They were lovers."

A look of shared understanding passed between Maggie and Lynn. "That explains so much," Maggie said.

"In fact, madly in love." Lauren handed over a small flash drive with a theatrical gesture. "We found letters hidden in our house, the same house where that picture was taken."

"They're all there on the flash drive," Jo said with rare emotion. "I helped Lauren scan them. Their entire relationship, from their first tennis game to sneaking all over the city for stolen moments."

"It's better than a romance novel," Lauren jumped in.

"But here's another layer to this mystery. Our Joelyn had access to some underground lesbian network," Jo continued. "She wasn't an innocent in all this. But the letters, as you'll see, are only from Eliza's side."

Lauren leaned forward. "You don't have Joelyn's letters on your end, do you?"

"Not that we know of." Lynn glanced to Maggie for confirmation.

"Maybe it's better that way," Jo said with a touch of sadness. "It doesn't end well. Your many-greats grandfather stepped in. Eliza married Henry, and Joelyn disappears from our family record."

"I was hoping they ran off to Paris together." Lauren smiled wistfully.

Lynn's expression darkened as she shook her head. "Eliza stayed married to Henry until the day he died. I'm not sure how happy the marriage was, though."

Lauren hung her head. "So that's it, then?"

I sat back in my chair, pulling myself away from the action. I, once again, had been only an observer in this conversation; however, the room was heavy with the weight of lives half lived and love denied. Sadly, it wasn't that far removed from what was happening in my present.

Lynn and Maggie shared another look, this one electric. Maggie nodded, and Lynn stood. "Wait here. There's something else. Let me go get it." She disappeared down the hall.

With the afternoon light filtering through the windows, we chatted about the condo that we already knew was part of the family residence. Decades before, it had been broken up and sold in pieces. Maggie lived two floors up and was thinking of selling. Her marriage had ended, and she wasn't sure, but she thought she might need a fresh start somewhere else.

Lynn walked in cradling a vintage art deco jewelry box and placed it on the coffee table between us. "When Maggie was eighteen and I was sixteen"—she began to paint her own type of reflection with her words—"our mother sat us down in the kitchen right here and gave us this box. We opened it and found two sets of identical diamond earrings. We were thrilled, and then, she told us that the real present was underneath. We tore into it, thinking more jewelry. Instead, we found this." She pulled out a worn envelope, its edges frayed by time. Written across the front in Eliza's now familiar script were the words: *To the people who will ask about Joelyn Steward.*

"What on earth?" Jo asked as if she couldn't believe her eyes.

"I know. It's astonishing, right? We didn't care about some old letter. As you can imagine, all we wanted to do was try on the earrings and dance about the kitchen. These were our first diamonds," Maggie added.

"Mom let us have our moment, and then she put the letter on the table and told us about our relative who'd died before either of us was born. Our mother had loved her with all her heart and remembered her quite well."

"She said Eliza was fierce, the kind of woman who could stare down a bull and win. Strong, stubborn, and never let anyone push her around. She said that once, when Eliza was young, she had let someone slip through her fingers. Mom said that regret forged her into steel."

"It was Joelyn." Lauren sighed, exhilaration shimmering at the edge of her voice.

Maggie nodded. "It fits, doesn't it? Eliza lived with our parents at the end. She passed away from lung cancer."

"I'm so sorry," Jo said. The empathy was back in her voice.

"Thank you. When she was diagnosed, the doctors had only given her a few months to live. She made it over two years."

"Too stubborn to let go." Lynn's fingers brushed across the box. "Our mom thought she was waiting. Waiting for something to happen, someone to come. She couldn't hang on long enough."

Lynn drew in a slow breath, her voice quieter now. "Our mom held on to the box for years, and when the time came, she passed it on to us with the same promise. What we didn't know was that our mother was also dying, another type of cancer, and that was why she passed it on so early."

Maggie picked up the story seamlessly. "It seemed silly and crazy. We loved our mother as much as she loved Eliza, so we listened. I remember thinking, this is a mystery for another day."

"We tucked the box away and, honestly, forgot about it," Lynn said. "I found it years later when I was cleaning that closet. My husband and I had moved in to take care of our father, and there it was, waiting patiently."

"That was about, what, five years ago? We toyed with opening the letter to see what was inside. There's something else there too. Pretty heavy. We wanted to see what could be so important that it would be passed down from generation to generation."

"But we'd promised our mom we'd keep it safe until the right people showed up."

Lauren's eyes locked on the envelope. "And here we are."

"This is…" Maggie shook her head. "I almost can't believe it."

No one said anything. We all looked at the box as if it was a message in a bottle cast into the waves of the future.

Their conversation was even more like watching a reflection. In this incarnation, I could hear them, even touch them if I wanted, but in a way, I was as invisible to them as I was to the people in the past. I used to believe the reflections pushed me away from people and life, but maybe I was the one holding the walls in place.

"A lot of things happen that you can't explain," I said quietly, trying to chip away at the wall. "Believe me."

Jo's eyes flicked to me, her expression sharp, or maybe that was just the way I was reading it.

I stood, putting more bricks in the wall. "I…I can wait outside."

"Are you kidding me," Lauren said and threw Jo a sharp look of her own. "None of us would be here without Hazel. She's the one who found the letters."

"Then she stays," Lynn said simply.

I sat back down, touched that Lauren had jumped in like a lioness to protect me.

Jo shifted uncomfortably in her seat. "Nobody was suggesting you leave," she said, her voice soft, almost apologetic.

Maggie picked up the letter. "Okay. So who does the honors?"

"It's your letter. You should open it," Lauren said.

Her hands steady, Maggie carefully pried open the seal. All our eyes locked on the fragile paper as she slid it out. And then, in a low and clear voice, she began to read.

The Letters

The Past: Eliza

My Dearest Love,
   Joelyn.
   To write your name again is so painful. I can't tell you how many times I stop to whisper your name into the emptiness of my day just to hear it said out loud again. I would give anything to say it to your person. That choice no longer exists, and that is something I will have to live with for the rest of my days. Mother and her new circle of friends have stopped gossiping about your family and your "illness," as they call it, but their voices still drip with sarcasm and jealousy. They speak of another poor soul's misery, but the rumors of you persist. That the pneumonia that brought such a hale and healthy woman down was something much more scandalous. They spoke of servants whispering of finding you in the bathroom, already cold and gone in a bathtub filled to overflowing. No matter what people say, I know what happened. I know that you died of the broken heart I gave you. That I had your fate in my hands, and I tossed it all away because I could not stand up for you, for us. It is all I can do not to follow you.

   I have thought about it more than I care to admit. Once again, my weakness holds me back. And the fact that I am with child. The baby inside me blooms while I wither. For her sake, I will live. I will give her your name. Henry will fight me tooth and nail. But I will win, and I will teach her to be strong and to live for her convictions and not for her fears. I will try to give her the gift that no one gave me. I hope that when she has a hard choice to make, she will make it easily, with love at her back. She will be our child, Joelyn, in name and in spirit. I will make you proud in death, even though I have failed you so very completely in life.

   I am not sure why I feel so compelled to write this letter. There is no one to mail it to. But I have the distinct feeling that someday, it will be read by the right people and that they will take a strength from it that I cannot. Whether this will be or whether I just want it to be, I do not know. All I do know is that after destroying myself in a world that was no larger than my own feelings and thoughts, I will now try to survive in a world where I live for others. Someday, when all that is done, I will find a way to return to you. This letter is a small step in that direction, although it brings me little comfort.

I love you, now and always.

Forever,

Elizabeth

CHAPTER THIRTEEN

The Present: Hazel

Lynn's voice faded, and it was as if all the air had been sucked out of the room. We were all frozen with the idea that the letter had implied.

Lauren finally voiced what we were too afraid to say out loud, "Suicide?"

"That's not her at all." Jo shook her head firmly. "From Eliza's letters, Joelyn didn't feel like a person who would give up. She would've fought for the relationship."

"I would have," I said, directing it to Jo. I didn't want to be on the outside looking in through the window at life anymore.

"What else is in the letter?" Maggie asked.

"Let's see." Lynn tipped the envelope, and the other half of the Christmas locket slid out.

The three of us gasped, although we should've been expecting it.

Lauren was positively giddy as she explained what the heart was and what it had meant to the couple. "The other half is up at Meerblick."

And there it was. We'd come to the end of the revelations again with no real closure. Maggie told Lauren to take the box, the letter, and the locket.

"That's a valuable piece of jewelry. We can't walk out with it," Jo, always the voice of reason, said.

Maggie shrugged, her expression resolute. "Our mother was very clear with the instructions. The letter and everything in it were to go to the *people who know about Joelyn Steward.*"

"We've followed her instructions so far. Why stop now?"

Jo was unconvinced. She finally gave them her cell phone, her parents' contact info in France, and practically all of Lauren's personal information as well in case they changed their minds. At the door, Maggie and Lynn gave us warm hugs.

"I'm going to take my time with these letters." Lynn held up the flash drive. "And then maybe can we come see Meerblick? See where it all happened?"

"Of course." Jo hugged them again. I couldn't help noticing that she was very free with her hugs with everyone else.

Later, I sat in the back seat of the silent Mustang, the box and the last of Eliza's secrets tucked in beside me. "What will you do with this box?"

In the passenger seat, Lauren shrugged. "I don't know. Any suggestions?"

I did have one. It had been tugging at me ever since Lynn had pulled the second half of the Christmas heart into the present. "This might sound ridiculous, but what if we...or you reunited the necklaces up at Meerblick. In the Blue Room?" That was the scene of their first intimate encounter, and it had produced the craziest interaction with the past I'd ever encountered.

"Isn't that a little cliché?" Jo said, glancing at me in the rearview mirror.

"Of course it is." Lauren twisted in her seat, her eyes sparkling with excitement. "But it's hokey in all the right ways."

With Lauren's support, I warmed to the idea. "Yes. Objects can be imprinted with energy, you know. Not scientifically provable." That was for Jo's benefit. "These necklaces, they're more than stone and metal, they're promises. Eliza said she'd never take hers off. If their love, the energy, if it's all strong enough, it may balance out whatever is going on in the house."

"Oh my God." Lauren practically danced in her seat. "Yes. We're totally doing this."

Jo's low hum was somewhere between resignation and acceptance.

"You know," Lauren said as if she couldn't stop herself, "I could frame one of the letters, add the necklaces, and hang it up in the Blue Room. Kind of a shrine to star-crossed lovers like Romeo and Juliet."

"Don't you mean Rosemary and Juliet?" Jo quipped, but at least she was playing along.

"That's perfect." Lauren beamed, her excitement bubbling over into wild plans, where she'd get the frame, what bakery she'd get the cake from, and who she'd invite. Us, of course, Maggie and Lynn, their grandmother. She even asked if Gran would come.

"She wouldn't miss it." I sat back against the seat, comforted that I'd see Jo at least one more time.

"Sounds like you're planning a wedding," Jo teased.

"I could do that too." Lauren's look swept over us both without further comment, but her meaning was clear.

Jo kept quiet. Good sign? I didn't know.

We pulled up to Lauren's house, and Jo drove straight into the driveway and killed the engine. What was I supposed to do now? Call an Uber to get home? As usual, Lauren was way ahead of me.

"Hazel needs a ride. She doesn't have her car with her."

"Oh." Jo froze in the driver's seat.

"You know where it is. Take her home. Use my car." She left no room for argument.

My shoulders tightened while waiting to see which way Jo would go.

Her fingers tapped the steering wheel once. Then twice. "Okay. Fine." She punched the ignition, and the engine came to life again, as did the spark of sudden possibilities.

I've replayed this moment countless times. How close was it to tipping the other way? When things went right, how close were they to going so very wrong?

Sliding into the front seat, I braced for the silence. Without Lauren talking a mile a minute, there was no one there to defray the tightness. Jo gripped the wheel, her knuckles stark white against the dark leather.

Then, she turned, her gaze locking with mine. For a moment, the tension was alive, crackling in the air. We spoke at the same time, our words colliding.

"Let me explain about Keera."

"Are you dating that woman?"

"God, no." My answer tumbled out as fast as I could shape it. "She's just my business partner. She handles publicity and bookings and all the financial stuff. I was out of the gallery up at your house, and she came over to talk about a business trip."

"Okay." Jo's hands relaxed on the wheel, color returning to her knuckles.

The atmosphere in the car shifted as if someone had cracked a window to let in fresh air. For a second, I considered leaving it there. I hadn't exactly lied, but I'd skewed the explanation to my advantage. Nope. Too much like the way Keera would have handled it.

I took a deep breath and jumped. "Okay. Full disclosure. We did date. Ages ago." Jo stiffened again. "Look, it didn't even come close to working out, and now the business partnership is falling apart. I've hired a lawyer to see if I can get out of everything with her." I winced at my words. Rushed and clumsy, as if Keera and I were in the middle of some quickie divorce.

Jo said nothing; in fact, her jaw clenched.

"Keera's a control freak." I tried again. "I make a lot of money for her, so it's hard, impossible even, for her to let me go. Believe me, whatever impression she gave you last night, all she was doing was protecting her investment."

Fuck, no better. Jo's focus stayed on the road.

"Okay. Yes. It's messy." My last attempt. "Maybe really messy once the lawyers get involved. But we're not dating, and I don't have any feelings for her anymore unless resentment counts. And last night, outside my place, before Keera showed up..." I paused, my voice softening. "That was almost the best thing that's happened to me in a very long time."

Jo glanced at me, one brow lifting in a question. "Almost?"

"I wish we'd kissed." As I waited for her to answer, heat, and not the good kind, flushed through me. My stomach twisted, and the following silence was maddening. It stretched long enough for me to replay every word and highlight each misstep with a neon light.

After what seemed an eternity, she reached over. Her hand touched my thigh, warm and steady. She squeezed gently, and my heart flipped like it had been caught in midair.

"I wish we'd kissed too," she said softly.

I covered her hand with mine, my fingers curling around hers as if to anchor this moment in time.

"You know it was those damn letters," Jo said, her voice noticeably lighter, "especially the one we heard today, that made me drive you home."

"Really?"

"Yes. Joelyn and Eliza had their chances stolen from them. By society and by their own fears. I don't want to live like that. Wasting all my chances." Her fingers tightened in mine.

"Thank goodness Lauren kept searching for the box."

Jo snorted. "Man, don't ever tell her that. She'll never let us forget it."

We both chuckled, a quiet, rich sound that settled something between us. We'd turned the page to begin a new story, our story.

Jo pulled up to my building. Her gaze darted around like she was scanning for trouble. Keera, most likely. To be honest, I might have glanced up and down the block as well. Thankfully, the street was quiet. Keera and her drama hurricanes weren't lurking in the shadows.

"There's a spot behind mine in the underground lot if you want to come up?" I tried to sound casual, but even I could hear my own nervousness.

"That would be nice," she said, a smile touching the corner of her lips.

I wished for a steamy elevator moment on the ride up. Where she pinned me against the back panel, breath hot against my skin, hands framing my face, and kissed me hard. Sadly not. I stood stiffly beside her, stealing sideways glances, trying to decode the quiet between us.

Here was the thing about me and relationships. I was terrible with beginnings, and clearly, endings weren't my strong suit, either. I lived too much in my own head. I hoped that Jo and I were moving forward, but so much of our time together had been two steps forward, a thousand steps back. That was an exaggeration, of course, but my chest tightened all the same. *Please don't let this night be another misstep.*

As soon as I opened my condo door, Jo made a beeline to the picture window where a silvery fog was starting to weave around the Golden Gate Bridge.

"Oh my God, this is gorgeous." She spun to face me. "The whole place. It's wonderful. So modern." She plopped on the sofa with an uncharacteristic flop. This wasn't the composed Jo I'd seen all week. This was someone letting her guard down. I loved it.

"Sometimes, I feel like I live in museums where the past feels heavier than the present. I guess that's another type of reflection." She paused and tilted her head, considering her statement. Her brows furrowed thoughtfully. "Right?"

"Yes. I believe that there are more kinds of reflections than just my kind." My heart did a little cartwheel. Jo hadn't said it outright, but I'd heard what she meant. *I'm trying to get it. I'm trying to understand you.* This moment was everything. It had never come with Keera, although I'd waited for years. From the beginning, Jo was trying to see me for who I was.

"That's why I chose this place," I said. "It's brand-new construction, fourteen floors up. No one has been in this space except me and the workers, I guess." I smiled nervously. "I haven't seen even one reflection. It's the best thing about this place."

"Right, you told me yesterday."

Shit, I had.

She didn't let me be embarrassed. "Interesting it would work that way. That makes it better for you."

"It does," I said and shifted my weight from one foot to another. Something between us had shifted too, like we'd cleared our first hurdle of the evening without even realizing it. "Do you want something to drink?"

"I'd love something. A glass of wine?"

I had another moment of panic. Jo had lived in France, the holy land of wine, and I relied on Dan, the cute guy at Trader Joe's, for recommendations that wouldn't break the bank. I did have his favorite Spanish wine in the fridge, so I grabbed that, threw some mixed nuts into a bowl, and brought both to the living room.

Jo had made herself at home on the sofa, her legs curled up under her like she belonged there. I chose the club chair across from her. Close but not too close.

She poured the wine and raised her glass in a toast. "To reflections."

"And letters," I added.

"And where the past can lead the future."

"Who knew?"

We clinked glasses. She took a sip and didn't spit it out. Instead, she twirled her glass in her hand, her gaze going distant. "I've been wondering, do you ever see reflections of yourself, or is it always of other people?"

The question sent a prickle up the back of my neck, not entirely unpleasant, but it did make me pause. It was a good question, a really good question, but was it too deep and complicated for right now? I took a deep breath and ran a hand through my hair. "No. Never," I said, my voice carrying the weight of all the years spent puzzling over my gift. "I wish I knew how this worked. I go all meta on myself, asking if a hundred years from now, will someone like me see moments from my life? Will they see me sitting here talking to you? It's a mind trip, and I know not the healthiest way to think about things."

Jo nodded, her gaze steady. "I know what you mean. Not healthy at all."

For a second, I thought she was judging me. Instead, she surprised me.

"I think maybe I created a reflection, not that I knew that at the time. But thinking about it now, I'm pretty sure I did."

The vulnerability in her voice made me sit up a little straighter. "Do you want to talk about it?"

She hesitated, her fingers tracing the rim of her glass. Slowly, she began. "Camille, my ex, was a runway model." Her story came out in bite-size pieces, gathering steam as she went. "We were happy at first. You see, she usually dated other models, and I was different. I was fine to let her bask in every spotlight. We moved in together, and like I said, it was great. She grabbed life by the throat and squeezed every drop out of it. I loved that about her. I'm a little more restrained. Keep things inside, if you haven't noticed."

"Not at all."

We both chuckled, the sound soft and intimate. The same way we had in the car when we were talking about Lauren. Was soft laughter going to be our thing? God, I hoped so.

"And then..." Her expression darkened as if she was living the moment rather than just telling me about it. "I don't know what changed. Maybe our life was too small for her. Maybe I wasn't enough."

I didn't even see how *that* was possible.

"One day," she slid her wineglass onto the coffee table, "I left for a work trip. I was at the station when I realized that I had forgotten a file I needed. I rushed back to our flat. I was gone for under an hour, and I walked in on..." Her lips pressed into a thin line before her words cut through. "I found her with another woman."

"I'm sorry, Jo." I wanted to reach out and touch her, but she was lost in the past.

She took in a breath and sighed deeply. "You know, when I tell people why we broke up, I always say, *another woman*. It's simple and clean. People hear it, and they get it. *Another woman* carries all the betrayal and hurt I felt at the time. But..."

I leaned forward, encouraging her but also giving her space. I knew better than anyone that some stories needed space to unfold, and I wanted to be the person in that space with her.

She rocked her head back and forth as she decided to continue. "But that's not what I saw. When I think about it, I see it like it's happening all over again. I see myself coming in like a tornado. I can still hear the door slamming against the wall as it opens. She's sitting on the couch, which, of course, faces the door. She's naked from the waist down, her head tilted back and her body arched up. Another woman is on her knees, her mouth right here."

She dropped both hands to her crotch.

"She's going at it like you wouldn't believe. Moaning and making so many other noises, I'm not even sure she hears me come in."

"Oh, Jo."

"I know. I know. But that's not even the worst part. I don't know if it's the noise of the door or if the energy in the room changed, but Camille raises her head and looks right at me. And she doesn't stop. She smiles. She drops her hand to the woman's head, holds her in place to keep going, and smiles."

Remembered pain flitted across her face, and she twisted her hands tightly together in her lap. "It was a horrible smile. I don't even know how to describe it. Triumphant. Dismissive. She knew she was breaking something fundamental between us and rubbing my face in it at the same time. And what's even worse, I just stood there. I didn't say anything. Didn't scream or cry or confront her. Just got my file and left. But inside…" On her lap, her fingers continued to fidget. "Inside, I was in this storm of anguish and betrayal and bitterness and rage. God, there were so many emotions at once. Way too many for one person to hold. I'm not sure I totally believe this, but maybe that's when I made a reflection?"

She went silent and dropped her head. I got it. The images she had painted were as sharp as cut glass in my mind. How did they live in hers?

"I'm so sorry." It was all I could say again.

Twilight crept into the room as the silence stretched out between us. It wasn't uncomfortable at all but necessary. Me untangling the threads of her story, her pulling herself back to the present. I'd have waited forever if she'd needed me to.

Finally, she raised her head and smiled thinly. "I wanted to tell you." Her voice was steady now. "Because you might be the only person who understands the difference between seeing memories and remembering them. I wanted to tell you so I wouldn't be the only one carrying this around anymore. It's so selfish. I'm sorry."

"No. I get that. You don't need to apologize."

"And I wanted to tell you because that this is the reason I've been so weird. Hazel, I liked you from the first minute you bent down to pet Edgar. But I've been hurt. It sounds like we both have, and I don't know if I'm emotionally ready for something new. But I'd like to push the past behind me and try. See where this could go?"

Her gaze met mine, hope and promise dancing together. And also, something I'd never seen in Keera's eyes: vulnerability.

"Oh, Jo. I would too. Try, I mean."

She let out a huge breath, scooted back into the sofa, and patted the cushion beside her. "Well, then. Do you want to come over here? You're too far away."

I wish I could say I moved with grace, but, no, I practically leapt up like a kid who had been picked first for kickball. Her laughter was warm and genuine. Mine too. And I knew for certain soft laughter was, in fact, our thing.

The rest of the evening unfolded with surprising ease. We ordered salads from a local vegetarian café that was also known for its cornbread and homegrown honey. Sitting on the couch next to Jo, I saw a whole new side of her. She came alive as we told each other stories of our childhoods. The physical ease with which she moved through the world was also a mental ease. Then she told me about the time that Lauren had scheduled two dates with two different boys at the same time in high school.

"Lauren's solution?" she said. "She convinced them both to take her to the same street fair. She ran back and forth between them, switching hats at various booths like a full-on Shakespeare comedy so neither boy would realize they were in a threesome."

"Did she pull it off?" I asked, popping a piece of cornbread slathered in honey in my mouth.

"You know, she did. Lauren comes off as ditzy, I know. Really, she's eccentric and razor-sharp when it counts."

"You don't have to sell me on Lauren. I'm a big fan."

"Me too." Her expression softened. "Her parents, my aunt and uncle, took me in when I wanted to stay in America for high school. That's when Lauren and I bonded. She opened her heart to me completely. That's her superpower, loving people without conditions, and I'll always be grateful for that."

"To Lauren." I raised my wineglass, now filled with sparkling water. Jo had asked to switch after her second glass since she was driving. She had an early appointment with the professor who ran the laser-plasma accelerator lab at Berkeley. I was a little disappointed, although I didn't know what I'd expected or wanted. Her not staying made the evening more comfortable since we both relaxed into the moment, knowing that it wasn't building to anything.

"To Lauren." She clinked my glass with her own, and a soft ding filled the air. "She practically pushed the kayaks into the river, didn't she?"

"Thanks for that, by the way. I'm sure teaching me couldn't have been that fun for you."

"Actually, it was. I liked how you connected to the nature around you. The water, the trees, even the wind spoke to you."

My pulse quickened with a soft warm current. Even then, she had seen me. "It does. I used to get out in it all the time. Now most of my shoots are studio shoots. I'm going to change that," I told her, but mostly I was telling myself.

We talked about my work a little. I told her about Atticus and the picture that had started it all. I almost told her about Edgar, but I wanted to surprise her at the gallery with the actual prints. She told me more about the lab she was visiting in the morning and the cutting-edge research with ion beams and energy that was going on there. I didn't understand much, but it wasn't lost on either of us that we both were connected to energy. Her voice became all warm and fuzzy as she talked about the science being done there.

It was crazy. We technically had only known each other for less than a week and had been through a lot of ups and downs in that time. But now there was the quiet, steady pull of something real.

And then the evening was over.

We lingered by the front door, reluctant to say good-bye. We traded small talk that went nowhere. Our words were placeholders for what should have been coming next. Then Jo, tucking a strand of dark hair behind her ear, asked softly, "Should we finish what we started?" Her gaze dropped to my lips and darted away.

I nodded, barely moving my head. She moved in until her face, her lips, were a heartbeat away. A shiver rolled through me. We were impossibly close but not touching. The air between us was electric with possibility, with a new future.

I tilted my chin up, closing my eyes in a silent invitation, and our lips met. Gently, tentatively at first. We didn't embrace. She didn't reach out for me. All focus was on the tender, trembling point of contact. Her tongue traced the contours of my mouth, and I lost myself in the play of her lips against mine.

When we parted, neither of us moved more than a fraction of an inch. Just enough to breathe.

"Hmmm." Jo's sigh was both happy and excited. "Worth waiting for."

"Not sure. Try again?"

"Yes," Jo said, but it was little more than breath as she leaned in.

This time when our lips met, desire leapt up in me like a lightning strike. She must have felt it too because her kiss turned passionate and urgent.

Jo made a small sound in the back of her throat, and the second I heard her moan, I needed her closer. I circled her waist with both arms and pulled her to me. Her breath hitched, and she slid her fingers through my hair. I angled my head, and Jo deepened the kiss. Our entire bodies were pressed together, and her breasts pushed up tantalizingly against mine. My tongue darted forward, nudging her lips. They parted almost instantly. She tasted like sweetness, from the honey at dinner and something sweet that belonged only to her. Then her tongue met mine, and something clenched inside me. Who knew our kiss would be like this? Hot and passionate and achingly sweet.

Jo's mouth left my lips and trailed soft kisses to the hollow above my collarbone. I arched my back. I had a flash of her descending lower, how my breast, my nipple would feel in her mouth, and as desire pooled in me, she pulled away. She looked at me, not into my eyes, but where her lips had been a few seconds before. Then she met my gaze.

"I should go." Jo bit her bottom lip. It was slightly swollen, and her eyes were dark and wide with indecision. "Yeah, I should go."

"Okay." I didn't want her to, but also, I wasn't sure I was ready to tap into all that passion and promise of our kiss. "Come by the gallery tomorrow. In the afternoon or whenever your Berkeley thing is done. I've got something for you."

"I'd love to. I'll text you when I'm on my way. Lauren finally gave me your info." She reached out to trace her fingers along my jaw. "I'm really going now."

We both chuckled. Yep, definitely our thing.

She opened the door, slipped out, and the evening was over. But with a little luck, *we* were at the beginning.

THE JOURNAL

The Past: Joelyn

I can't wait.

I slide my hands under the thin straps of your nightgown and pull gently so one side falls off your shoulders and then the other. Here in the silvered moonlight, the nightgown falls to the ground and pools around your feet. My breath catches. You are naked before me, vulnerable and radiant. The air between us sparks and shimmers. My heart forgets to beat. You are so slender and so beautiful standing there in front of me—I can see your emotions all over your body—the rapid flutter of your pulse at your throat, your lips quivering, your breasts rising and falling with each quickening breath. My hands almost lift of their own accord. You are soft and warm beneath my palms. You gasp and arch into my touch with a grace that makes my heart stutter. I groan, raw with longing, and step out of my nightgown. I watch it flutter to the ground to lie intertwined with yours. You stare, frozen, and I guide your hand to my breast. Your touch starts as gentle as butterfly wings but grows bolder as I move against you. Your breath comes heavily, filling the room, matching the urgent rhythm of my own. I lift your fingers to my lips and press another kiss to your palm. I lead you to the bed, each step cementing the promise of us. We find our way together in the soft darkness on the cusp of something magnificent.

I can't wait.

CHAPTER FOURTEEN

The Present: Hazel

"Hazel, did you hit the lottery or something?" Franklin, the barista at my favorite coffee house, asked me the next morning as he handed me my coffee.

"No, why?"

"Because you're glowing. Something must've happened."

I grinned ear to ear. "Yeah, but not the cash kind."

"Oh my God. You're dating someone!" He slid a second cup across the counter.

"Too soon to tell." But the grin didn't drop off my face.

He winked at me and gave me a thumbs-up. "The love lottery beats the money lottery any day."

Franklin was right. I'd woken up full of sunshine. My lips still tingled with Jo's kiss. I practically skipped the rest of the way to work.

Inside, Lana was already organizing a cabinet of posters that Cherry had unsurprisingly left in horrible disarray. I handed her the coffee with a flourish.

"One oat milk latte."

"I can't believe you remembered my order."

"Keera made you run out for coffee way too often," I said with a shrug. "We got a pretty good machine after you left, but I still like the way they roast their beans at Brewed Bliss. At least for the morning."

"Still."

"I'm happy you're here, Lana."

"Me too."

We tapped our cups together in caffeinated cheers, and I headed to my workspace. At my desk, I pulled out the notebook where I'd been scribbling my plans for the live mascot project. Seeing the messy sketches and half-formed concepts made my pulse quicken. This was the kind of work that could make me happy. But as I flipped through the notes, my excitement began to fizzle.

A new project like this had a million moving parts. I knew what to do for the photographs. I'd maybe a thousand ideas but had no road map for how to get there.

In the past, this was where Keera would've swept in. I'd toss her the big picture, and she'd shoot it down, not profitable enough. We would've argued a bit, and eventually, she would've huffed and puffed to her office to grudgingly figure out the logistics. Sure, in the end, it would have cost me several celebrity shoots and other unnamed favors, but she would've made it happen.

I leaned back in my office chair and let the truth settle over me. Dreams needed structure, and structure didn't come naturally to me. Honestly, if I took away all the drama, Keera was an excellent producer. With a sigh, I closed the notebook. Maybe I needed to back burner the idea until Keera and I had come to some sort of new arrangement. Damn. I hadn't thought this through. Like most people, Keera wasn't all bad. It was the way I was looking at her.

The morning flew by in a blur of productivity. I pulled a crumpled to-do list out of my desk, the kind filled with doodles and good intentions. Crossing things off was satisfying—editing photos for new marketing materials, updating the photos on the gallery's website—the kind of stuff I told myself I'd get around to but never did. Every few minutes, my eyes darted to my phone. Jo was still in her meeting, and I knew better than to expect a message. Still, I checked. And checked again. Finally, I exiled my phone to the other side of the room, dropping it onto the flat file cabinet. Out of sight, out of mind. Or at least I hoped.

I was walking away when a memory tugged at me. On impulse, I reached for the bottom drawer and opened it. Inside were photographs of the local river otters that I'd taken ages ago, tucked away like forgotten treasures.

I pulled out the one on top. *Outfishing the Fisherman.* I smiled, remembering when I'd stumbled on the otter. I'd crouched and luckily had a long lens on the camera. He stood on a shallow riverbank, the early morning light glinting off the rippling water. A fisherman's tackle box with colorful lures sat open next to him. In the background was an open thermos of coffee still steaming, as if the fisherman had just stepped away. Even though he hadn't seen me, the otter had posed almost proudly, standing upright on his back legs, one paw gripping a fish he had snagged from the nearby bait bucket. In the photograph, his chest puffed out, and his whiskers perked up in satisfaction. His cocky little grin said, clear as day, *work smarter, not harder.*

I dug deeper. I'd forgotten about *Whiskers and Whispers.* Two otters, whiskers almost touching, sat by their den. Water droplets clung to their fur like tiny jewels. One leaned into its friend, a paw positioned as if it was cupping its mouth to whisper. The other stared at the camera wide-eyed, as if letting the viewer in on the juicy secret.

I sifted through more photos, moments that felt awfully like reflections came flooding back. A mother lovingly scolding her cubs, an adolescent stretching out in an impressive yoga pose, and two friends sharing food as if they were at a picnic. They were undeniably adorable, so much so that Keera had even called them *sickeningly cute* when she had seen them originally. But as I studied the images now, something clicked.

There was a show here. Not only about otters but about us. These creatures in their joy and mischief, tenderness and cleverness, mirrored so much of what it meant to be human. What if I went back to the river and captured others but in a more raw, natural state? What if I juxtaposed their playful world with a more traditional one and asked the question, which was their real world?

The idea danced around in my head. This show could be exactly what I needed: a project to anchor me as I worked through my arrangement with Keera and waited for the live mascot calendar to gain momentum. At the very least it was something to think about while I was not checking my phone every ten seconds for a text.

It was well past lunch, and the butcher block was covered with a dozen otter photos when my phone finally dinged. I snatched it up and tapped the screen.

Done with Berkeley. Headed your way.

Three red hearts popped up right after.

I tried to brush it off. It was just an emoji. Everyone used them. It didn't *have* to mean anything. But three hearts? That had to be better than the green checkmark or the car emoji, right? A flutter of nerves spread through me. What was the right response? My fingers hovered above the keyboard, determined not to overthink but failing miserably.

See you soon.

Should I add an emoji? Maybe a heart too? Something more original? I froze in indecision. Groaning out loud, I flipped the phone over on the file cabinet without sending anything extra.

From that moment, I was utterly useless. My productivity fell off a cliff. I checked my reflection in the bathroom mirror. I double-checked Edgar's prints, making sure they were in the order I wanted. Then I rearranged the otter photographs for something to do.

When Lana poked her head into the workspace, I jumped like I'd been caught doing something embarrassing. "Hazel, there's someone here to see you. Her name is Jo. She says she's a friend?"

I grinned, which gave everything away.

"Oh, damn, girl. She's super cute," Lana said.

"Isn't she?" I said in a giddy rush. "What did she think of the gallery?"

"Well." Lana paused, enjoying every second of teasing me. "She came in, looked around, and…"

"Lana, come on. Help me out here. We're brand-new."

"Okay. Okay," she relented with a laugh. "She gasped a little. In delight."

"Really?"

"Really. I'll go get her."

Moments later, Jo walked in with her usual poise and effortless confidence. I could watch her move all day. She was smiling and pulled me into a quick, warm hug. "Oh my God, Hazel." She stepped back, her hands lingering on my arms. "The gallery is amazing. I didn't know the pictures would be so…I don't know. Alive and interactive. That's not quite right, but I feel like every single one of the animals is talking directly to me. Like this guy right here." She motioned to *Outfishing the Fisherman*. "It's like he's mid-sentence about to say something cheeky. How do you even do that?"

I shrugged, shy under her admiration. "Seriously. No idea. It's the good part of the gift."

She leaned closer to the photo, her brow furrowed as if she were decoding a secret. "How does it work?"

I fiddled with the edge of the butcher block. "It's like with the reflections. I'm seeing something others don't. Not just what the animal is doing but what they're feeling. The camera channels that."

Jo's gaze softened, her eyes warm as they held mine. "Well, whatever it is, it's incredible."

Not for the first time, her words, her validation, settled on me like a welcome warmth on a cold day. I tried not to let it show how much it meant to me. I pointed to the butcher block. "I'm thinking about a new show. Going back to my roots. Away from the celebrity animals."

She walked the length of the butcher block, scanning the other photos. "It'll do well. Who doesn't love otters? And like I said, these are incredible."

I lingered behind her. Probably too close but I didn't care. "Enough about me," I said, trying to shift the focus. "How was your meeting?"

She turned, and we were inches apart. Neither of us stepped back. Testing the closeness, maybe. Seeing if it still felt right after last night. It did to me. "Interesting." Her voice dipped. "Weirdly, my trip may have given me some insight into your gift."

"Really?"

She nodded.

"Tell me. In small, simple words, though. I'm not a science person."

"Okay," She laughed and lifted a small gold bag that she had been holding. "Small words coming up. And this will make it go down easier. I brought treats from my favorite French bakery in Berkeley."

That was thoughtful. I loved the way she always carried a piece of her world into mine. As if she knew what I was thinking, she leaned in and pressed a quick kiss to my cheek. It was sweetly impulsive but also planting a promise for something more. Before I could say or do anything, she stepped back, her movement casual, as if she hadn't just knocked me off-balance.

We spread out on a nearby table, and she pulled out two pastries in clear plastic containers. "These are almost as good as your photos."

"What are they?" They looked delicious.

She pointed to the first, a pair of crispy golden rounds with dollops of cream between them. "This is a Paris-Brest. That's praline cream. It's meant to look like a bicycle wheel. Someone made it for a bike race between Paris and Brest over one hundred years ago. And this"—her hand hovered over a sleek, chocolate-covered rectangle—"is a gateau opera with almond sponge cake soaked in coffee syrup with ganache and coffee buttercream."

I leaned closer, taking in the delicate pastries. "They're stunning. Edible art."

"They taste even better than they look." She pulled two forks from the bag and handed me one. I knew I overthought things, but I waited to see if she was going to pull plates from the bag, if she was going to cut each dessert into neat halves, or if we were sharing out of the plastic containers. She flipped open the lid of the opera cake, speared a bite directly from the container, and popped it in her mouth. "Dig in," she said around her mouthful.

I did, my fork sinking into the rich layers. Sharing like this, randomly grabbing a bite with no rules or pretense was intimate. If I were looking for signs of where this relationship was going, this was a good one.

The flavors of the cake hit me. "Oh my God. It's kind of tastes like tiramisu."

"But better, right?"

"Yes. Definitely better. What can't the French do?" I took another bite. "Okay, sugar's kicking in. Lay your theory on me."

She tapped her fork against the edge of the container before she spoke. "As you know, I work in plasma physics. Stop me if I'm telling you anything you already know. I don't want to mansplain."

"Don't worry. You won't be."

"So Dr. Cosman runs a large plasma device lab, and they're doing so many fascinating experiments in low-temperature plasma, like fabricating semiconductors at the atomic scale."

I laughed self-consciously. "You've already lost me."

"Okay. Let's just say, it's a cool place."

"That I understand."

"Good." She smiled at me, not unkindly, and took another bite. "When I was there today, I was watching the plasma light up all bright orange in the plasma-processing machine. Basically, when electricity is applied, electrons jump to higher energy levels. And when they fall back down, they release photons of light at specific levels. And it causes a flash of color from the plasma."

"Hmm." I licked praline cream from my lips. "And how does that relate to me?"

She sat up straighter, bristling with excitement. "Again, this is only a theory and probably a bad one at that. But what if when people are in these intense situations, like stress, excitement, whatever, they release chemicals and hormones? Like adrenaline. That rush of chemicals can create electric currents in the body. It's why your heart races, why your breath quickens."

"I get that," I said, narrowing my eyes, trying to find a footing in her words.

"And electricity? It's moving electrons."

The connection snapped in my mind. "And you think that for some reason, I can see the light and images that the electrons leave when they fall back down."

Her fork hovered over the last bite of the opera cake, and then she slid the container to me. "It could be possible. When we were up at Meerblick, you said something about auras. They are, from what I read, from the people who believe in them," she added for good measure with a playful tap of her fingers against the metal table, "electromagnetic radiation fields that surround a physical thing. In this case, one person. They call it the visible blueprints of your thoughts. Maybe you can process that information."

"How?" Gran and I had, of course, talked to several *experts*, but not one of them had ever taken my gift as seriously as Jo was now.

"Who knows? Maybe it's genetic. Some anomaly in how your eyes or their connection to your brain works. Maybe something to do with your rods or cones. Some people can see more colors, and animals can see in the dark. You have reflection vision."

I chuckled. "We're going to have to get a better name if you want it to sound like a superpower."

Her laughter, warm and bright, joined mine. "Let's table the branding for later."

"So you're doubling down. Not ghosts." I'd never thought they were, but it was nice to be on the same page.

"Yes. Lauren is going to be crushed. She was talking podcasts. She wanted to call it *Two Hot Ghouls*."

"That doesn't even make sense."

She answered, her tone deadpan. "That's Lauren for you."

I arched a brow. "Who are the hot ghouls?"

"Her, of course and…" She shifted her weight in the seat and leaned toward me. "You, naturally."

I could feel the words climbing out of my mouth. *You think I'm hot?* Instead, I cleared my throat and went with something safer. "So where do you stand on the reflections now?"

She tilted her head, considering. "I believe in them as much as anyone who can't see or feel them."

That was a start. I stayed quiet, hoping she'd continue.

"I can't explain how you knew about the letters in the wall of the Blue Room. And now, maybe, there's some actual science behind it. Not quite as fleshed out as I'd like. But it's a working theory."

I bit my lip to keep the flood of emotions from spilling out. It wasn't fair to unload years of Keera's doubts and skepticism on her.

She looked at me and shook her head.

I steeled myself for whatever was coming next.

"But you know what? None of that matters as much as the one

thing I know for sure." She met my gaze, her voice steady. "I believe in you."

My throat tightened. "You do?"

"I do." She dropped her fork on a napkin, clasped her hands on the table, and leaned forward. "You and your crazy experiences have shown me that there are all kinds of reflections, and I don't want to be stuck in mine, circling around Camille, trapped in the past. You've made me realize that I want to look forward. To a future where the reflections, only the good ones, are yet to be made."

"That's a wonderful way to think about it."

"And I hope to explore that future with you."

The air between us shifted, becoming something electric and undeniable.

"I don't want to scare you off," she added softly, like she was confessing. "I'm a scientist. I need clarity and data. I'm not great going in blind."

I reached across the table, brushing her fingers lightly. "I'm not scared. I'd like that too."

It was more than the truth. Thanks to the reflections, I'd been an observer for so long. With Jo, I could stop being a bystander in my own life.

The silence that followed wasn't heavy. It was alive with possibilities. She leaned in even closer, and in the space of a heartbeat, our hands moved toward each other until the edges of our fingertips overlapped.

"Oh my God. I've got a gift for you." In a whirlwind of activity, I jumped up and grabbed a folder from my desk. I led her to the butcher block and placed the folder down in front of her.

"What's that?" she asked. Her voice carried a teasing edge.

With deliberate care, I pulled the first photo from the file. It was Edgar in full stride, bounding through the golden oat grass near the house. His tongue lolled out in a wide, joyful pant, and his ears flew back in pure, unbridled excitement. The coastal light bathed him in a hazy, dreamlike glow. The image hummed with motion and life.

"What the..." Jo gasped and covered her mouth with her hand. "Oh my gosh. When did you..." She was at a loss for words.

Her emotion tugged at something deep inside me. "That night after kayaking and before dinner."

"I knew you had a camera up there, but, Hazel, this isn't just a picture. It's alive."

"Wait. There's more." I pulled the next one from the folder. Here, Edgar, off-center, was caught in a moment of absolute stillness, his nose lifted to some unseen scent. His fur shone with the same ethereal glow, and the oat grass that surrounded him was soft and out of focus, looking very much like a living halo.

Jo exhaled sharply. "It's like he's thinking. I wish I could hear his thoughts."

I pulled several more from the file, spreading them across the butcher block in a private show. Her eyes never left the images. She didn't just look at them, she absorbed them.

And finally, the one I'd been saving for this exact moment. My hands trembled as I placed it in front of her. Edgar was sitting in a classic dog pose: his front paws forward, his head tilted, his body angled in a gentle, eager posture of complete attentiveness. He was gazing beyond the frame. His eyes, liquid and luminous, were the focal point of the image and shone with an almost human-like intensity of love and devotion.

"Hazel," her voice cracked, "what's he looking at?"

Here was the moment I'd been waiting for ever since I scrolled through the pictures on the SD card. I met her gaze and forced myself completely into the moment. "You." The word was little more than a breath.

Her eyes widened. "Me?"

"Yes. You had come out to call us in for dinner. Edgar was already in the frame, he saw you, and I took the picture."

Her fingers lightly touched the edge of the photograph as if she couldn't believe what she was seeing. Eventually, she turned to me, her eyes shining with something I couldn't name but felt deep in my chest.

"This is how much Edgar loves you."

She could barely choke out her response. "I only ever see him from my perspective. You've given me his story."

"That's all I've ever wanted." I swallowed against the tightness in my throat. "To tell the stories that no one else sees."

"You've done that. And I'm not just talking about these." She held a finger over Edgar on the butcher block. "I'm talking about everything. I'm beginning to realize that there are stories everywhere."

"There are," I whispered.

She reached over and took my hand. She lifted it to her mouth and dropped a gentle kiss on my knuckles. "Thank you," she whispered. Her lips parted, and the tip of her tongue darted out to moisten her lips.

Something within me clenched in anticipation. "You're welcome." Even I could hear the longing in my tone.

Thankfully, she leaned in and kissed me.

So much of my life had been spent in the background observing, sitting back, and watching things happen even when they were happening to me. But this kiss? Whole different ball game. I was one hundred percent in the moment. All my senses were alive, buzzing, demanding.

I felt it all. Her warmth, the softness of her lips, the faint taste of coffee. Our lips teased, nibbled, and caressed, and my world narrowed to only Jo.

Her hand slid from my waist and caressed its way to the nape of my neck. Once there, her fingers rested lightly on my skin. Her touch first prickled and then burned. A ripple of heat shivered down my spine. A shudder chased it, and I couldn't stop the low groan that escaped me.

Her hands twined up into my hair, pulling at my curls with a gentle passion. Then her mouth drifted to my cheek, where she left a trail of soft electric kisses. Down, down, until she reached a spot above my collarbone. A playful nip followed by a slow suck. I let out a shaky breath as her lips lingered there.

Her breath tickled my neck before she kissed her way back up. When her lips found mine again, the kiss deepened, deliberate and unhurried. I darted out my tongue, and her mouth parted instantly. She tasted even sweeter than she had the night before. Partly, it was the cake, but I had a feeling that she'd always taste like dessert to me.

A sharp voice cut into our private moment. "Is this all you two do?"

We broke apart, not like guilty teenagers but slowly, like divers surfacing from deep water. In a small act of defiance, I hoped, Jo kept her hand on my arm as we turned toward the door.

One hip propped against the frame, Keera came into focus. Her arms were crossed and her gaze cold enough to freeze the room. "I heard from your lawyer," she said when she was sure she had our attention. "I didn't think you would move so fast."

Jo shifted and stood up like a shield, rising to her full height beside me. No question about it. She had my back this time.

Keera took her time stepping into the room, her heels clicking deliberately on the cement floor.

I took a second to clear my head and said, "I'm serious about renegotiating."

"I can see that." Her tone was deadpan, but her eyes flitted to Jo. It wasn't curiosity; it was strategy. She was calculating her next move as if it were a championship chess game. "Serious about it now or later?"

Jo jumped in to answer before I could. "You two can talk now. I need to go anyway." She turned to me, and the shift in the room was subtle but complete. Keera faded into the background, her presence irrelevant. "I need to get home to walk Edgar. And we've got a family dinner tonight." She paused, and her gaze locked on to mine with a private light flickering behind it. "But if you're free tomorrow, there's this place in Fisherman's Wharf. They make the best chocolate soufflé you'll ever have." She waited for my answer as if we were the only two people in the room.

I nodded and wanted to make more of a show. "Yes. I'd love to."

"Great." She leaned in to whisper in my ear. "Wild horses, lawyers, or ex-girlfriends can't keep me away. I'm all in."

Jo bent a bit farther and kissed me on the mouth. There was no passion to it but something even better. Possessiveness. The message was clear, and it wasn't for me. *She's mine.*

Under her kiss, my lips curled up in a small, unintentional smile. Despite everything, I didn't want Keera to feel bad I was moving on. For all our wreckage, I wanted us to have a new healthier relationship, something we'd never managed before.

Jo broke from our kiss and reached for the photos of Edgar, her fingers curling protectively around the edges.

"No. Don't take them," I said quickly. "Let me frame them for you."

"You don't have to do that."

"I know. I want to," I insisted. "Don't worry. Only a few."

"Okay. Thank you." She handed the photos to me. "Tomorrow." One word. But it was solid, like a promise. Maybe even a lifeline.

She scooted around Keera who, of course, didn't move an inch to get out of her way. I watched her leave, still feeling the warmth of her lingering kiss.

Keera cleared her throat, dragging me back to the cold edge of reality. "So you're really going through with this?" She held my gaze a beat too long, as if testing me. I didn't look away.

I stood so we'd be on an equal level. "Yes. I am." I was beginning to realize that sometimes, letting go of the past was facing it head-on. Jo had it right. Nothing was going to pull me back now.

"Termination is a little extreme."

"Maybe." I swiped a hand through my hair. I wasn't one hundred percent sure that was what I wanted, but I added the second thought out loud. "What we have here isn't working for me anymore."

She raised her palms in the universal symbol for, *what the hell is wrong with you?* "We're making money hand over fist. Why not ride this train until the wheels fall off?"

"The money's great," I said with a shrug. "But I'm not happy. I told you. These celebrity shoots? They're empty. My art needs connection. Real connection. You can't fake that."

"You're a wonderful artist," she said, throwing me a bone. "But come on. They're just pictures of animals. Famous animals, not famous animals, what's the difference?"

"It's not the animals, Keera. It's what happens between me and them." I paused, searching for a way to explain it to her. How could she not know after all this time? "The celebrity shoots are like walking through a beautiful forest with your eyes closed."

She said nothing. I went back to language she'd understand.

"Look, I'm not saying I don't like the money. I *like* the money. But it's supposed to buy me freedom, not tie me to projects I don't care about. There needs to be a balance. Projects you want and projects I want."

Her continued silence thickened the air. She wore her poker face, a look I'd seen before when she wanted me to backpedal. To crumble. It seemed absurd to think I'd grown a spine in the last week, but I guess one day, I stood, scared, at the edge of a cliff, and then the next day, for various reasons, I could fly.

She finally broke the silence. "And what exactly are the projects you want?"

I took a breath and laid my thoughts out cleanly. First, the river otter series, returning to the river, the time and cost it would take. Her mouth twitched in distaste, but she didn't interrupt. Then I mentioned the live mascot idea. I spun it as something flashy with a marketing angle built in, focusing on a real role for her.

When I finished, she pursed her lips. "There might be something there," she said carefully, noncommittal. "But honestly, I'm not sure I want to move forward in this way."

I recognized her play immediately. She was creating leverage and forcing me to reevaluate my position.

I didn't bite. "Your call. That's the point, Keera. We both get to choose. And we both need to be happy with those choices."

"True," she said, her tone purposely casual. "I'll think about it and get back to you."

Without waiting for my reply, she spun on one heel. The clicking on the cement echoed ridiculously, almost like gunfire, as she exited. I let out a breath. The ball was in her court now.

My phone rang, vibrating against the butcher block table. Gran's name lit up the screen.

"Hey," I picked up the call, "how'd you know?"

"Know what?"

"That I had my first ever adult conversation with Keera."

"Ah." She drew the one word out, and it was so full of love and relief that I knew how worried she had been about me. "And how did that go?"

"Just started. We're still in it. She was feeling me out. Seeing what my bottom line is."

"Typical," Gran added with a knowing hum.

"To be fair, we both were." I let that settle as the realization sank in. "You know, I'll be okay with whatever happens. If I have to regroup, I can. She has more to lose than I do."

"Damn right, she does." Her tone lightened. "Now, tell me about Jo."

I did. Not the steamy details about the kisses, but there was enough in my story to communicate I was smitten. She teased me in that wonderful way only a grandmother could.

After we hung up, I went out to the gallery to see how Lana was doing. The summer was alive with activity. Tourists wandered in, drawn by the warm weather and the buzz of the season. I hated to admit it, but the Suki Lush photos were pulling people in. A family huddled around the GloFish photo, and their youngest child of five or six announced loudly, "I'm getting a fish like that!"

Lana, ever the people person, caught my eye and waved me over. "Everyone," she said, "this is the artist."

The way she said it, with pride, caught me off guard. Cherry would've never done that in a million years. Questions flew at me from all directions.

"What is Suki Lush really like?"

"How many tattoos does she have?"

"Does she have diamonds on her appliances?"

"Does she pay people to wait in line for her?"

I surprised myself by laughing and telling a few choice, appropriate stories. The small crowd ate it up, hanging on my every word. By the time they filtered out, their hands were full of merchandise. Keera was right about one thing. I couldn't completely walk away from this part of the business.

Two stragglers stayed behind. Obvious out-of-towners, the couple had matching cable car T-shirts and fanny packs. The man approached first and asked in heavily accented English, "Are you the photo taker?"

He held up a gallery brochure and pointed to a picture on the back where my hair was behaving. I could see his confusion. I smoothed down my curls. "That's me."

His companion smiled brightly. "I like you very much," she said earnestly. "I meet you on the internet. We come here to see your pictures."

"Thank you." I didn't know if she meant the gallery, San Francisco, or the whole country. Whatever the case, I was flattered.

"I love the dogs." She pointed to Suki Lush's Jack Russell terrier staring out of a frame along one wall. "You do too."

"I do. Very much. Come with me."

At a cabinet near the back rooms, I slid open the doors to reveal unframed prints lying in various slots. I ran my hand down the spaces until I reached the one I wanted. I pulled out a full-sized print of Atticus, my childhood dog and, in retrospect, my first muse.

It was the same print that had changed everything when I'd showed it to Keera all those years ago. For a long time, I couldn't look at the photo without feeling a sharp pang. First, because Atticus was no longer with me, and then because Keera was also no longer with me, at least romantically. But now, as I showed it off, all I felt was love.

Love for the dog who'd taught me how to love dogs and all animals. And love for the dog who had shown me the path I was still walking.

The woman must have seen the emotion on my face. "This is the dog you love," she said with certainty.

"Yes. I loved him very much."

She touched me briefly on the arm for comfort, and to my surprise, I found myself rolling up the print and slipping it into a nearby mailing tube.

"On the house." I handed it to her.

She froze like a dear caught in headlights on a mountain road. She obviously didn't know what I meant.

"It's a gift. From one dog lover to another."

"For me?" Her hands hovered over the tube like it might vanish.

"Yes. Please take it home," I said. "Only if you want."

She wrapped me in a tight hug. "Thank you. Thank you."

As they walked out, the woman clutching the mailer like a treasure, Lana appeared beside me.

"That," she said, her voice warm with approval, "was a nice thing to do."

I watched the door swing shut behind them. "Sometimes, it is not about selling the art. It's about sharing the love behind it."

She glanced around the gallery as if she could see all the potential and nodded.

I put my finger to my lips. "Shh. Don't tell Keera."

THE JOURNAL

The Past: Joelyn

This is right.

We lie together on the bed, exploring each other with hands and lips. Each touch is a revelation. Each caress uncovers new wonders. You gasp as my mouth finds you in all of your intimate places. The way you move beneath me ignites something primal and tender in me. I want to possess all of you. I move in, but you surprise me, gently pressing me back against the sheets. Oh, your lips! I thought I knew their magic from your kisses...this is transcendent. I can't believe that your lips feel better than they did on my mouth, but they do. I moan and grab your face in my hands. You smile. Truly smile. Your eyes light up with joy...with longing... with love. My heart stumbles in my chest. In this moment, I feel connected to everything. To the universe itself. What is happening between us pulses like a living thing. The energy radiates outward in golden waves. Filling every corner of this room only to come rushing back to us. It lifts us higher and higher into realms that I never knew existed. It drives me to lose all control. To go places that I have never gone with another person. We are trembling on the edge of something magnificent and terrifying.

Nothing could be more right.

CHAPTER FIFTEEN

The Present: Hazel

Later that night, I sat cross-legged in bed, my phone balanced on a knee. The screen glowed against the dark room, and my thumb hovered over my keyboard. I was caught in a classic spiral that in the past would've had me overthinking well past midnight. Should I text Jo? Or should I wait for her to text me?

She had mentioned there was a family dinner, and I didn't want to interrupt. Then again, she also didn't have to answer it right now.

Time to stop overthinking things.

I'm going to bed soon. You want me to meet you at the restaurant tomorrow?

She texted right back. *I'd rather pick you up at 6. Made a reservation.*

I'll be outside. Can't wait to see you.

Me too. Followed by a heart emoji.

I didn't have even a second of hesitation before I texted two hearts back to her. I flopped against the pillows, grinning at the ceiling. Would heart emojis become another one of *our things*? I would've gagged if one of my couple friends had told me that heart emojis were their thing. But here I was thinking they were super cute.

The next morning, when I unlocked the gallery door early and stepped inside, a low murmur of voices drifted through the space. I froze. Someone else was here.

The sounds came from the back where Keera's small office was tucked away. One voice was hers, sharp and familiar. The other, a woman's I didn't recognize, came from a speaker. Keera hadn't bothered closing her door; no doubt she thought she'd be the only one here this early.

I turned to go, and then I heard my name.

I should've stepped outside or slipped into my own office and shut the door. But I didn't. I strained to hear every word.

"I'm coming off like the royal bitch. It's not fair," Keera said. Anger and resentment spiked through her words.

"Are you telling me that you don't want to be a bitch?" The other voice was calm and contained. A friend? A mentor? A therapist?

Keera let out a dry laugh. "Well, if I had to list three adjectives at a job interview, bitch wouldn't be on the application."

"That's not what I asked," the voice pressed.

Keera sighed, the sound heavy, as if she was thinking about the question. "I don't know. There are times when it comes in handy."

"Like when?"

"Like at the beginning." Her tone was defensive but honest. "Hazel had no idea how to structure a business. Being tough was a good, efficient strategy."

Dammit. She wasn't wrong.

"And now you're at disappearing acts and high-powered lawyers," the voice said.

So it was a therapy session. The woman even knew about my retreat to Meerblick. Good for Keera. I was so glad she had someone to talk to.

Keera didn't reply right away, and when she did, her voice was low and bitter. "I can't believe she wants to renegotiate the contract. I tried to do right by her. You'd think Hazel would be smart enough to realize that if I hadn't pushed her, if I hadn't supported her for years, she'd be nowhere."

Fuck. The words hit me like a gut punch. *Nowhere* was pretty harsh, but if I was being honest, I wouldn't have made the leap to photographing animals without her. I'd planned to make my living with nature beauty shots.

"You could be right. Maybe she would've gone nowhere. But here's the problem. She's somewhere now. And you can't handle her the way you have in the past. To move forward, you need to see her as a straight-up business partner. A true equal in whatever comes next. Are you capable of doing that?"

"I don't know," Keera said quietly, almost as if the words had slipped out without permission.

"Do you even want to?"

This time, there was such a long pause, I thought the call had disconnected.

Finally, Keera spoke. "I think so."

Wow. I would've bet hard money that she would've said no. A weight in me loosened, and a gentle realization washed over me. Keera hadn't been the only one boxing our relationship in a corner. I'd done my share of the damage. I'd been jealous, refusing to deal with my insecurities, and definitely passive-aggressive. That couldn't have been easy for her, either.

"I'm glad to hear that," the voice said. "Despite how you may have molded Hazel or pushed her into a wonderful career, she's her own person. You two grew out of a relationship, and now it looks like she, at least, is growing out of the partnership."

"I know," Keera said, sounding what? Resigned? Accepting? Forward thinking?

"What you need to figure out is what you want now. And I'm not only talking about Hazel the business partner, the moneymaker. I'm talking about Hazel the person. When you can answer that question, you'll know how to move forward."

"Hazel the person..." Keera repeated, her voice trailing off. And this time, I could identify the emotion. Sincerity.

Embarrassment and shame surged through me. I shouldn't have been listening. True, I'd heard what I needed to hear, but this was a moment Keera deserved to have without an audience. Unbelievably, she was doing the hard work to figure our issues out, maybe even more work than I was doing. Respect flickered through me as I slipped across the floor, careful not to make a sound. I let myself out through a side door so the front door chime wouldn't give me away.

I'd been lucky to come in when I had. To hear Keera's side of the story in a way where she wasn't shaping it for my benefit. This had almost been a reverse reflection. Hearing and not seeing. Present and not past. And yet, this reflection, as all the others did, gave me more of the story. Not that I was endorsing eavesdropping.

I walked to Brewed Bliss, although the last thing I wanted was another cup of coffee. It would, however, give Keera time and space to finish her conversation and hopefully digest it in a good way. But honestly, I needed to sit with what she had said too, and I might as well do that at the coffee shop.

I took a table by the window where Franklin had just replaced the yellow daisy in the vase. It looked at me, fresh and hopeful.

I found ways to kill time. It started with a photo of the cinnamon heart on my cup of coffee to Gran. Then I switched gears and popped in my earbuds to listen to a highly rated paranormal podcast. I wanted to see what Lauren might be going for with her *Two Hot Ghouls*. Lauren was important to Jo, and I liked her too. She was smart, passionate, and endlessly entertaining.

After that, I people watched, answered other texts, and generally caught up on my life. Then, to my horror, I remembered my promise to Cherry. I'd been so preoccupied that I'd done nothing about it. I scrolled through my contacts and found Robbie, a friend from college who was now doing fashion photography for catalogs. I fired off a quick text asking if she knew of any modeling agencies or gigs that might give Cherry a shot:

She's very pretty but a little eccentric. She'll have to sell herself. Any leads? Drinks on me and I'll spill the whole wild story.

Satisfied that I'd at least taken a step, I headed back to the gallery at ten fifty. Lana was already behind the register juggling a phone call with her wonderful efficiency. I handed her a coffee and headed to my workroom. The door to Keera's office was firmly shut, and I slid into my own space as if it had been my first visit to the gallery this morning.

I spent the rest of the morning, not that much of it was left, shuffling around the otter photos, leaving spaces for more photos. I pasted sticky notes with a written idea of what would be my dream shot in the blank spaces. At one point, I looked up to see Keera standing in the door frame, much like she had been the day before, arms crossed, one hip against the threshold. But something was different. The sharpness that had been in her eyes was gone, replaced by something quieter. Thoughtful, considering, not aggressive at all.

"Hi," I said, feeling very self-conscious.

"Hi," she replied evenly.

"Everything okay?"

She gave me a long and pointed look. "Yeah," she said with a small nod and went back down the hall.

Interesting. We'd said practically nothing, and yet, maybe everything?

I was equally surprised when later I headed out to the gallery to see Lana and Keera quietly talking. Not close in a romantic way, I was quick to note, but in that way where each was being super careful.

Keera's voice was calm. "Let's create a schedule that fits for you. I'll make it work on my end within reason."

Lana nodded, relief obviously flooding over her.

I took a step back to let Keera do her job. Could things be taking a turn for the better?

And then, Jo rushed in like a whirlwind. She looked frantic. "Oh, good you're here," she said, her voice a mixture of urgency and panic. "We have to go to Meerblick. Right away. Lauren says the house is freaking out."

❖

Once again, I was making the long drive up Pacific Coast Highway, this time with, thankfully, the good driver of the Steward cousins. Once again, Jo's hand rested on my thigh, grounding me despite the obvious agitation that was riding with us in the car.

"I've never heard Lauren sound so unnerved. She couldn't even explain exactly how the house had freaked out."

"Believe me, it's hard to explain."

"Sure, but it's Lauren. I've never heard her at a loss for words before. She's at the nearby bakery waiting for us. Can you text her and tell her we're on our way?"

I did. Lauren replied almost immediately with one word: *Hurry.*

I held up the screen for Jo to see. "Why did she go up there in the first place?"

"You know Lauren." Jo sighed and drummed her fingers lightly on the steering wheel. "Last night at dinner, she was going on about the letters. She was getting pretty worked up about how the societal constraints of the time created the tragedy of Joelyn's and Eliza's relationship."

"She's not wrong. It was awful."

"On that, we all agree. Even Uncle Mike said how relieved he was that times have changed for the better. That we didn't have to hide or lie to the people we love anymore." Jo's voice softened. "He meant it, and I'm sure he said it for my benefit too. But it upset Lauren."

"Why?"

"She felt that her dad didn't see Joelyn and Eliza as real people. To be fair, he hasn't read the letters or seen the reflections as you have."

I glanced at her. She said *reflections* as if it was a fact, not a theory, and my chest tightened in the best possible way.

"And he's also in science. Medicine. He shifted the conversation to my lab visit, probably without thinking. But Lauren was hurt. She felt like she was the only one taking this seriously."

"So she left?"

"She texted me this morning saying that there was no way that Joelyn committed suicide. She couldn't let it go, especially when everyone was brushing it off. And she was going up to Meerblick to prove it."

"She didn't want you to come?"

Jo shook her head and squeezed my leg. "I think she wanted something of her own. She might be a little envious of us. We're getting closer, and she and I spent a lot of time at Meerblick after Camille. She talked me down from some dark places. She even had a theory that my emotions back then, all that hurt and anger, filled the house with energy and set all this in motion." She glanced at me, clearly self-conscious. "What do you think?"

I shook my head. "I wish I knew." The answer was certainly getting old, but it was the only one I had. "Suicide doesn't feel right to me, either."

"I've been thinking about that. Eliza was not Joelyn's first rodeo."

"You think she was out and proud?"

"As much as anyone was back then. We only saw Eliza's side of the relationship, but to me, Joelyn relentlessly pursued Eliza from the beginning."

I nodded. "Eliza did give her plenty of outs in those first letters. The chance to dump their friendship before it even got started."

"And Joelyn ignored every single one of them. She was the one who organized all the innocent dates, from the baseball game to the movies and the illicit rendezvous when things got serious. Even hearing about it secondhand, she comes off as the one calling the shots."

I couldn't argue with that.

She was on a roll. "All these things point to a different ending. One where Joelyn heads up to Meerblick and waits for Eliza to come back from South America. Then, when she does, they find a way to be together. Or Joelyn doesn't wait and goes off with another woman."

"Either would have been better." But my mind went to Clarissa. I remembered the anger in the reflection. She had thrown the letters with withering disappointment and fury. From what I saw, she might have been too overwhelming a force to fight. "Maybe Joelyn couldn't face her mother. For all her forward thinking, a lesbian scandal might have been a bridge too far in the twenties."

"Maybe," Jo said, though she didn't sound convinced. "Joelyn was her daughter, and if there's one thing my family has, it's strong backbones."

"Really?" I teased. "I hadn't noticed."

Jo laughed, shaking her head. "Yes, really. Strong enough for Lauren to race up there alone and then demand that we come up when things went south."

"I'm with Lauren on this," I said, leaning back in my seat. "We should be together. I don't like all these mysteries, either."

"Can we get some answers when we get there?" She looked at me, and before I could even open my mouth, she answered for me. "I know. I know. You've no idea."

We both chuckled. Yep, definitely our thing.

❖

We picked up Lauren at the bakery as they were locking the doors. She sat on a low stone wall near the entrance, her arms wrapped around herself like she was holding everything in. The moment she saw Jo's car, she jumped up and hurried to us. Jo parked, and we both got out. Without hesitation, Jo walked over to Lauren with her arms wide open.

"We're here," she said, pulling Lauren into a close hug and holding her there.

When Jo let her go, Lauren turned to me, and I stepped in to hug her as well. "Both of us are here for you." I wanted to make sure she knew that I hadn't come only for Jo. Her grip on me tightened, her head dipping slightly against my shoulder.

"I'm not going back," Lauren said tremulously as we stood moments later in the emptying parking lot. "At least not until tomorrow. I don't want to get stuck there in the dark."

I raised an eyebrow but didn't argue. From my experience, reflections—or energy, if that was what we were calling it now—didn't care about the time of day. They came when they wanted. Lauren needed to feel she was in control, though. So I let it go.

"We'll find a place in town." Jo patted her shoulder reassuringly.

"Thanks." She bit her lip and looked at each of us. "You're not going to believe what happened at the house. Let's find a hotel, and I'll tell you the whole story."

As it turned out, most of the places were booked thanks to the summer weather and a nearby music festival. We finally found a room at the Tea House Lodge that was on the far edge of town and, despite the name, only had coffee in the rooms. Lauren told us that she didn't want to be alone, so we all crammed into a double queen room.

Later, we sat cross-legged on the beds eating Chinese takeout. The smell of orange chicken, garlic eggplant, and spicy noodles filled the air. Lauren stabbed her plastic fork into one carton with more force than necessary.

"Dad kind of pissed me off last night." Jo glanced my way with a knowing look but didn't interrupt. "He was treating Joelyn and Eliza like their story was over."

"Their relationship did end one hundred years ago," Jo said carefully.

"Sure, that part did. But that doesn't mean it's over." She waved her fork just like Jo while she spoke. "I drove up here with Eliza's part of the necklace. I thought I'd reunite it with Joelyn's, as Hazel said, and give them a tiny part of the happy ending that they deserved."

Jo handed me the carton of dan dan noodles she was eating, and I smiled at how easily she shared food. I loved this beginning part. It was magical, discovering all the little quirks about someone and realizing that they made you like them more.

"I know," Lauren continued. "It's dumb. But you two were getting together. You are getting together, aren't you?"

Jo and I looked at each other and nodded at the same time.

"That's great." Lauren put her carton on the bedside table and pointed at Jo. "You're a perfect couple. And I knew that before you even met each other."

"Fair, but what does that have to do with Joelyn and Eliza?" Jo asked.

"Nothing. Everything. Point is, I'm a great matchmaker. Even if the match is in the past. As silly as it sounds, I thought I could do the same for Joelyn and Eliza."

Jo opened her mouth, and Lauren raised her hand. "I thought if I put the pendants together, something would happen. Okay, I'm going to come clean. Driving up here, I had a little fantasy about putting them together so I could see the reflections like Hazel."

I understood all too well about driving up Pacific Coast Highway with fantasies swirling around my head.

Lauren took a deep breath. "When I got to the house, I put the key in the door. Something was wrong. It didn't feel stuck exactly, more like something was pushing back from the other side, almost as if it was waiting for me. I forced the key in and opened the door. And that's when it started," she said. "It hit me like a ton of bricks."

"What did?" I asked softly.

"Your energy. Your force field...I don't know...your gift?"

I froze with a fork of noodles halfway to my mouth. Was that possible? Could Lauren have felt the energy? I'd never met anyone else who could, but that didn't mean it wasn't possible.

"How did it feel?" Jo asked. She leaned forward and met Lauren's statement with an open, direct gaze.

Lauren nodded, and I smiled at them. At us. We were finally all on the same page. United by belief as we charged wherever this new revelation would take us.

Lauren struggled to speak. "It didn't feel alive at all. Okay, if you repeat this, I'll deny it."

Jo raised an eyebrow, amused, but stayed silent.

"It wasn't them. It wasn't a ghost. But...whatever it was did feel angry. Battered. Wounded, even. I'm probably just projecting now after the fact. But, I swear, it was telling me something."

We waited for her to continue.

"It told me to go upstairs. To the Blue Room. There weren't words or anything. but I had to go. As if I was being pulled by a riptide."

"And..." Jo pressed, impatient, leaning forward again.

Lauren exhaled. "And when I got there, something was telling me to look in the hole again. Ridiculous, right? Both Leo and I had searched it twice, but I couldn't shake the feeling. The flashlight was right there on the bed still, and so I looked." She paused, and a flicker of something—nervous delight?—flickered over her face. Safe with us now, Lauren was enjoying the performance of it all.

"Lauren." Jo prompted, trying to keep her on track.

"Right. Okay. I found this." She reached into the backpack at her feet and pulled out a weathered leather journal. The initials *JLS* were etched onto the front cover. "This. It's Joelyn's. A diary or thought book or something. It was crammed deep into a corner. I have no idea how we missed it, but we did."

"Maybe it wasn't ready to be found," I said, again realizing that I had no idea how any of this worked.

She took a deep breath, and her voice sharpened. "Well, it was ready yesterday because the second I pulled it out, all hell broke loose."

I sat straight up. I knew how quickly that room could turn.

"The energy," she said, eyes wide. "It was everywhere, buzzing, jabbing at me, turning, me inside out. Is that what you felt?"

I nodded.

Lauren's eyes snapped to mine. "It was horrible, wasn't it? I had a much more romantic picture of what went on. I thought you sat around watching ghosts or movies of the past. I had no idea it could attack you." Her voice broke, the delight in the story evaporating. "I didn't know if I'd make it out."

"But you did," I said gently. "You were strong when it came at you."

She nodded resolutely.

"If it makes any difference," I offered, "I don't think it's really coming after us. Not in a personal way. It just feels like it is."

Her laugh was bitter. "If that's your gift, Hazel, you can have it."

I didn't know what to say to that.

Thankfully, Jo cut in with the one question we should have asked first. "What's in the journal?"

Lauren looked at the book in her hands. "I don't know. I was too freaked out to look. I just grabbed it and ran." Without another word, she opened the cover and scanned the first page.

"Holy shit! It's sex. Hot, intimate, mind-blowing sex," Lauren shrieked. "I think this is Joelyn's and Eliza's first time at Meerblick!"

"Clearly," Jo said after Lauren handed her the book. "Eliza alluded to it in her letters, but now we're getting it from Joelyn's perspective." She passed it to me.

"And she's not holding back," I added.

When Lauren started reading Joelyn's words out loud, Jo turned to me, but the second our eyes met, she ducked her head. A blush crept up her neck, blooming across her cheeks. It was so endearing. I knew why she was embarrassed. If things progressed and we were lucky, this could be our story. That wasn't lost on either of us. What she didn't know, though, was that I had already seen it, lived it in a dream so vivid, it burned. Every sentence brought back the raw electricity I'd felt that night. Each line was a live wire of memory and longing. I also dropped my head but for very different reasons.

I forced my myself to look up. Screw embarrassment. There was nothing shameful here. Joelyn hadn't been ashamed. Neither was Lauren. Why should we be? What Joelyn and Eliza had shared that night wasn't just passion. It was connection, deep and consuming. A flame that burned across time. *We should all be so lucky to know a moment like this.*

Thanks to Joelyn's journal, we did. Lauren's voice breathed life into the past. Together, she and Joelyn were painting the night in details so rich, it felt like we were all there. Watching. Remembering. Feeling it. It was the best kind of reflection. Shared by the three of us.

"Love is forever," Lauren finished softly. She closed the journal with reverence, sighed, and said, "That was so beautiful. They had true love."

"Yes." I willed Jo to look at me. Our gaze met, and I glanced to Lauren to bring her into the moment. "And let's be honest. Pretty damn good sex."

"We should all be so lucky." Jo's eyes never left mine.

"Well, you and I, Jo, got it in our blood." Lauren waved the journal between us. "This is our legacy." For a moment, we all just stared at each other, then laughed out loud. The tension broke. Lauren tucked the journal back into her backpack. "To tomorrow, then. Let's go back and take that house by storm."

I worried there might be some awkwardness the closer we got to bedtime. But there wasn't. Lauren took the takeout boxes to the trash outside, giving me and Jo a moment alone. While she was gone, Jo produced a bathroom kit filled with a toothbrush, toothpaste, and a comb.

"The front desk sells them," she said, holding out two kits. "You want red or blue?"

"Blue," I said, taking it gratefully. Then, as if reading my mind, she handed me a T-shirt to sleep in and a change of clothes for the next day. "They might be a little big, but I was hurrying."

She had thought of everything.

"Thank you for coming," she said, stepping closer to me. Her voice softened with her sincerity. "You didn't even hesitate when I asked."

"Are you kidding? I wouldn't miss this for the world."

She took my hand, raised it to her lips, and kissed the inside of my palm, her way of melting me completely. I leaned into her, and we stood there for a long, quiet moment, soaking in each other's presence.

"This isn't how I imagined our first night together," she murmured, her forehead resting against mine.

"Me neither," I admitted.

"When Lauren finds out that she was a part of our first sleepover, she'll never let us live it down. Although, in a way, we've already had a lot of activity." I imagined she was referring to the journal.

"Hopefully, we'll have another night just the two of us." The words tumbled out before I could stop them. My cheeks warmed. When had I become this bold?

"Count on it." She brushed her cheek against mine like a promise.

The door clicked open, and we broke apart as Lauren came back in. I slipped into the bathroom, my heart still racing with my hopes and dreams for the future. Alone, I texted both Gran and Keera, telling them where I was and that I needed at least one more day. Gran would worry, of course, and Keera? I was trying to be a good business partner, the kind someone didn't need to be a bitch with.

When I emerged wearing an oversized T-shirt that read *Wanted Dead and Alive—Schrodinger's Cat*, Lauren and Jo were already sprawled on one of the beds, laughing at something on Lauren's phone. The other bed was for me. No awkwardness there, either.

I woke up in the middle of the night and turned to watch Jo sleeping on the bed next to me. The room was bathed in silver moonlight, and her breathing was soft and steady. Maybe I imagined it, but I swear there was a smile at the edge of her lips.

I'm dating someone who smiles in her sleep.

That thought kept me awake longer than it should've. What part of it, I didn't know. That I was dating Jo or that she was someone who smiled in her sleep? Both worked for me.

We all woke early, a sense of purpose pulling us into the day. We took one car, and Lauren, back to her usual self, prattled nonstop on the drive to Meerblick.

"We're like the Three Musketeers," she said from the back seat. Without discussion, she had given me the seat next to Jo. "Or the Fellowship of the Ring. Hazel, you're Gandalf because you have powers. I'm obviously Frodo. Jo, you're Legolas."

I snorted and exchanged an amused glance with Jo. "Legolas, huh?"

"I'll take it." She smirked, her eyes on the road. "He doesn't leave footprints. Although I don't know what that gets me."

As soon as we rolled up to the house, Lauren grew quiet. She wasn't the only one. My apprehension built too. If the energy was as strong as she said, we could all be in trouble.

Jo parked the car and climbed out first. Her movements, as always, were steady and smooth. She moved up the porch and tried to push her key into the front door. "She's right. Something is in there," she said, struggling. "I can't get the key in."

"Push?" I said, not actually thinking it was good advice.

Jo gritted her teeth. "It's like pushing into rubber cement." She twisted the key harder. "Oh, there it goes."

The lock turned with a reluctant click, and she tried, unsuccessfully, to push open the door.

"It's still there," Lauren said quietly from behind us. It wasn't a question.

Jo exhaled sharply. "There's definitely something pushing from the other side." The muscles in her back tensed as she planted her feet, her hand braced against the doorknob. "A little help?"

A shiver ran up my spine, prickling my scalp. Even so, I moved up the steps to stand with her. I cupped my hand over hers on the doorknob. As soon as our hands touched, a sharp jolt of that all too familiar energy stung my palm.

"Ow." Jo yanked her hand back and shook it out. "What the fuck was that?"

"You felt it too?" I whispered with awe.

Lauren rushed up onto the porch, her eyes wide. "The house. The energy," she said, her voice trembling but certain.

"That was only a very small part of it," I said.

"Shit." Jo flexed her hand. "That's unbelievable. No wonder you spent the night on the porch. Actually, it's a good thing you both got out."

"Welcome to my world." I shook my head, doubting anyone would want to join me.

And then I froze. Had I stumbled onto something? Were Jo and Lauren tied to this too? From the beginning? This new energy thing had never been only about me. Lauren had said that it started when Jo had brought her heartbreak home from France. And I'd felt it for the first time after Jo had touched me before she'd entered the house. Could she be the key? A least for me?

"We should try this again," I said.

Jo stiffened. "You sure?"

"Yes." My voice steadied as I looked at her. "I'd like to test something. Could we have created a path that allowed the energy to flow?"

Jo bit her bottom lip. "Like a circuit." Her eyes narrowed slightly as the wheels turned in her head. "Are you asking me if you're a resistor?"

I blinked. "I have no idea what that means."

"Sorry. You could regulate the flow of energy from the house or anywhere and provide a specific voltage for the reflections." She nodded and overrode her hesitation. "Yes, that's sort of what we talked about yesterday. It still tracks."

"But it isn't just me," I said. "You're a part of it too."

Jo ran a hand through her hair, her fingers lingering on her neck as she no doubt tried to piece it together. "Maybe I'm the place where the energy flows to."

I half shrugged. I was still a little lost.

"I ground you." Jo nodded as she spoke.

"Holy shit." Lauren jumped up and down behind us. "I knew it. You're her anchor. You balance the energy."

"Can we try something?" I extended one of my hands to Jo as an invitation.

She didn't hesitate, twining her fingers with mine. Together, we stepped back to the door. "You first," I said, pointing to the knob with my free hand.

Her eyebrows lifted in a question, and I nodded. "I have no idea what's going on, but this might work."

She dropped her hand on the knob, and I covered it with mine. Holding hands twice over, we formed a perfect, unbroken bond. The instant our hands touched, the energy on the other side surged toward us. Almost like a muscle car, it revved up and took off, shooting through the knob and into us.

This time, I didn't try to fight it. I gripped the knob tightly, but mostly, I hung on to Jo. I let the energy slide through me, swirling in a way I couldn't describe. It wasn't alive, but it sought something, a balance, a connection, a charge to complete the circuit.

Jo's breath hitched beside me, and we moved as one, pressing the knob down. The door opened with a quiet pop sound, like a vacuum seal breaking.

Lauren crept onto the porch to look over our shoulders. "It's still there. I can feel it."

"It is," I said simply.

Lauren edged closer, wedging between me and Jo. "So are we going in?"

I wasn't sure. I stared into the depths of the hallway, feeling the energy still pulsing within. Opening the door was one thing, stepping inside was another.

But I wasn't the same person who had stood on this porch days ago, paralyzed by fear and uncertainty. Today, I'd come back with a new weapon.

Control.

Not over the energy but over myself: my relationship choices, my art, my gallery.

Maybe, if I was being honest, quasi-control.

But that might have been enough for the house.

Still holding Jo's hand, I reached to grab Lauren's too. "The Three Musketeers," I said softly, more to myself than anyone else.

Taking a deep breath, I led us inside.

The moment we crossed the threshold, the energy slammed into me like a tidal wave.

Stupidly, I'd thought I was ready. I'd planned to welcome it, to embrace it the way I'd accepted the spark at the door. But this was a raging tide, surging with a force designed to pull me under.

The impact was immediate and overwhelming. The energy rushed into me, tearing through my thoughts with ruthless efficiency. The energy unleashed every emotion in me. Intensity, longing, and desire rolled through me. But this time, they were accompanied by something sharper, something that cut straight to my core. Pure, gut-wrenching agony.

It wasn't only sadness or pain. It was so much more. As if there was no hope left in the universe. It consumed me, swirling through my mind, rushing into every thought and crevice.

My knees buckled. The world tilted beneath me, and I fell, physically to the floor and mentally into a great void. Panic clawed at my chest, and I cried out, my voice raw and desperate.

Jo caught me.

Her arms wrapped around me with protective fierceness, pulling me close and anchoring me against her body. The agony that had been tearing through me receded like a wave rolling back out to the sea.

"I got you." Her words touched me to my core and became a mantra as she held the storm at bay. "I got you. I got you."

Oh my God. Jo is my armor, my real gift.

There was real power in a true connection. We fit together seamlessly or close enough. She balanced me like opposite charges linking to neutralize the chaos. My mind began to clear.

With Jo sharing the burden, the edges of the energy separated from my mind. It was no longer tangled with me.

Holy shit. This might be something I can control.

Tentatively, I reached out, my mind brushing the edges of the force. It was jagged, frayed in places, but I didn't flinch. Slowly, I scrambled along its boundaries, feeling for a grip. I found an edge and latched on to it.

I can do this.

I began pushing the edges together, forcing them closer despite their resistance. They fought me at first like stubborn magnets refusing to meet. But I kept pushing, kept focusing until they finally touched. I folded it in on itself until it was no longer a sprawling chaos but something heavier and more compact.

With a forceful shove, I threw it back into the hallway, leaving me trembling but intact.

From somewhere behind me, I heard Lauren. "Look. The air is shimmering."

I saw something different.

The hallway wasn't empty anymore. It was teeming with Joelyns, dozens of her, darting in and out of view in echoes of the past. Each carried a deep well of emotion: laughter, sorrow, anger, with her as she moved.

I sucked in a sharp breath. *I did this.* I'd found the control to pull these reflections into the present. Imprints that had been hiding beneath the surface waiting for a path to emerge.

My gaze landed on one Joelyn moving across the hallway. She was clearer than the others, her form sharper and more vivid. The weight of her presence chased the others away, and in a heartbeat, they blinked out of existence, leaving only her.

She wore the sheer nightgown that I'd seen in my dream, and her body was hunched and defensive. But it wasn't her posture that broke me. It was her expression. A deep sadness was etched on her face.

In her hand, she held a letter. No. *The* letter. I recognized it immediately. It was the last letter Eliza had sent. The one where she'd told Joelyn that she was no longer hers, the same crumpled, well-read one from the den. This was the letter that had cost her everything.

She moved to the staircase and began to climb, each step heavy with despair. I stepped out of Jo's embrace to follow. The second Jo's arms loosened around me, Joelyn flickered out of existence on the bottom stairs.

"Wait." I reached back, my hand grasping for Jo's.

"She's caught a reflection. Jesus, Jo, grab her hand."

Jo's warm fingers slid into mine, grounding me again, and just like that, Joelyn reappeared two steps higher on the staircase.

"Come on," I said, pulling Jo with me as I too, began to climb.

We followed Joelyn's slow, plodding pace. Jo's hand in mine steadied me, and together, we climbed up the stairs and into Joelyn's final story.

Joelyn turned into the Blue Room. She crossed to the dresser where the silver box currently in the den waited for her in the past. This version on the dresser was pristine and new; the two lovers sitting under the palm trees gleamed in shiny silver. Joelyn flipped open the lid, revealing the letters tied in the bright red ribbon. With deliberate care, she buried the one in her hand at the bottom of the pile.

I stood frozen, mesmerized. I'd never seen a reflection like this, so long, so vivid. Usually, they were brief, fleeting moments isolated in one location. But this? This was Joelyn's life unfolding in real time. And that wasn't even the craziest part.

When Joelyn moved, the room shimmered and transformed. Within two feet of her body, the space became the world she had inhabited in 1925. Furniture shifted, fresh flowers appeared in an empty vase, and a neatly folded quilt popped up at the edge of the bed. Beyond that small radius, the room remained as it was in the present, a bizarre split of past and present.

Behind me, I could feel Jo and Lauren. They made the only sounds I could hear. Lauren's excited murmurs were quickly silenced by Jo's firm shushes. I blocked them out, narrowing my attention to Joelyn.

She carried the box to the wall where we'd discovered it days ago. Around her, the shimmering, transformative energy restructured the room. Joelyn opened a built-in cupboard that wasn't there in the present and pushed on the back panel. A secret compartment only a little bigger than the box popped open. It made perfect sense now. When the room had been remodeled, no one had bothered to look behind the cupboard.

One mystery solved.

Joelyn closed the cupboard door with a heavy hand, and my heart stuttered. This felt final, like she wasn't coming back. And sure enough, she crossed the room, heading to the attached bathroom.

I hesitated, unsure if I should follow her somewhere so private, but Lauren pushed up against my back, and we all three crammed into the bathroom doorway. Joelyn spun the taps on the tub. Water, silently without a sound, spilled into the porcelain.

Holy Shit. My stomach dropped. *This is what Eliza wrote about. This is where she kills herself.*

Panic flared in my chest. I gripped Jo's hand so tightly, I was afraid that she might lose circulation. She didn't pull away. Instead, her other arm circled my waist, anchoring me. "I'm here," I heard as if from a great distance, and she gave me the strength to keep watching.

While the water continued to run, filling the bath, Joelyn sat on the closed toilet, her head in her hands, her shoulders shaking with silent sobs. When she eventually got up, tears still streaked down her face.

My heart broke alongside hers. I desperately longed to reach through time to comfort her. To tell her that broken hearts mended, sometimes stronger than before. That she didn't need to do this. That there were other ways to gain closure to her love affair with Eliza. But, of course, I couldn't. I was powerless to stop what was coming.

Once again, I was forced into the passive observer. My usual role.

Joelyn wiped away her tears as her expression hardened with resolve. She dropped her nightgown and stood naked before me.

I gasped, stunned by her raw beauty. Like an ancient Greek statue, she was magnificent, all sharp lines and soft curves, a vision of strength and vulnerability. She was so achingly alive.

She rolled her shoulders back and took in what could only be described as a cleansing breath. Then she stepped over the enormous lip on the tub and into the water.

I grabbed the doorjamb with my free hand, not wanting to watch what came next but unable to turn away. I was stuck in this moment as much as Joelyn was. Getting into the tub, she slipped. Her foot caught on the edge, and she tripped sideways. Her arms flailed widely, searching for a hold and found nothing. Her head came down hard on the porcelain, connecting violently at the right temple. Her neck snapped sideways, and her body collapsed into the water. Facedown. Her hair fanning out around her like a dark halo.

Joelyn's lifeless body floated in the water for only a heartbeat longer before jerking back into the past. The bathroom snapped back to the present, the tub empty, the nightgown gone. Jo and Lauren were staring at me, their bodies tense with a thousand unspoken questions.

"No," I sobbed. Jo took me into a deep hug.

Once again, her warmth wrapped around me, and I let myself melt fully into the present. Lauren stood nearby, uncharacteristically quiet, though she bounced lightly on her toes, waiting.

I met her eyes. "She didn't kill herself."

Lauren gasped, her hand flying to her mouth.

"She slipped and fell," I continued. "It was an accident. She didn't give up. Not even close."

"I knew it," Lauren said softly and climbed inside the hug with me and Jo.

❖

Afterward, we tucked ourselves back into the den with the letters, the journal, and the new truth we'd uncovered. The energy was still there, but the room was quiet, almost reverent, as if the house or the past was listening.

"You know," Lauren said, her legs curled up under her in the club chair. "Joelyn would've waited for Eliza to come home. And somehow, some way, they would have been together."

"They could've gone to Paris like you wanted," Jo said. We sat on the couch together, not quite touching but close.

"Exactly." Lauren nodded eagerly, full of her usual exuberance. "Joelyn wouldn't have given up."

"No, I saw her face," I said, the memory of Joelyn's resolve upstairs still vivid. At the time, I'd thought it suggested a terrible decision, but in hindsight, her resolution pointed to an emerging strength. "She would've found a way forward," I added with certainty.

We let the unfolding versions of the past hang in the air for a few moments, all of us picturing the alternate lives that Joelyn and Eliza might've had if tragedy hadn't intervened. Her life had ended too early, but at least it wasn't at her own hand.

Lauren broke the silence. "Do you still feel the energy?"

I reached out, testing my new control, trying to sense if there was energy in the room. There was a hum, like the power of a storm in the distance. "Maybe a little?"

Lauren tilted her head, curiosity lighting up her face. "And before Meerblick, you never felt it?"

"No, just reflections. They popped up randomly. Like little bursts of emotion."

"I bet you'll be able to interact with them more now. Maybe you'll always feel the energy before the reflections now or maybe force the energy into the reflections?"

I took a deep breath. "I'm wondering about that too."

"Right." Lauren nodded. "Can I be there when you test it out?"

"Geez, Lauren." Jo patted my thigh in solidarity. "Give her a break."

I placed my hand over Jo's, squeezing lightly. "You might both have to be there." I glanced at them both. "I was stronger with both of you beside me."

"And I saw a shimmer of light or a spark of static electricity. Maybe you can share your gift?"

"Maybe," I said, more to appease her than out of conviction. My mind was racing with bigger questions. Could I control the reflections now? Could I summon them on demand? Was this morning the exception or the new rule?

Lauren, as always, was running ahead of the conversation. "Think of the possibilities. We could travel the world giving comfort and closure to people. Maybe we could even work with the police to solve crimes. This could change everything."

Oh God. I groaned inwardly. I could never introduce Lauren to Gran. They would have *Three Hot Ghouls* streaming on Spotify before I could blink.

Jo smirked as if sharing my thoughts. "Let's finish this chapter before you write the sequels," she said, her tone more affectionate than reprimanding.

"That's right." Lauren bounced out of her seat and bounded out the door. "I came here to unite the pendants. Eliza's is still in the car. I'll go get it."

As she darted out, Jo swiveled to me. "You're stuck with both of us, you know."

"I do." I smiled. "But for the record, I'm not touring the country or starting a podcast."

"Don't worry." She smiled back, and it went all the way to her honey brown eyes. "I guarantee you, Lauren has already moved on to a reality TV show."

I laughed, although I was pretty sure she wasn't joking. Then I voiced a thought that had been gaining traction for a while. "Can I be honest with you?"

"Always."

"I'd love to explore the energy and reflection connection more. But not in the way Lauren hopes."

"No?"

I shook my head. "For as long as I can remember, these reflections have defined me. And not in a good way. They've pushed me into the background as an observer, so much so that sometimes, I'm not sure who I am."

"Oh, Hazel." Jo rubbed a hand down my arm.

Once again, she centered me in a way that I could have gotten used to very quickly. "It's not that bad. But I liked when earlier, I controlled the energy. When it did what I wanted rather than me sitting back, watching whatever it wanted to show me."

"I totally get that."

"Thanks." I paused, not knowing how she'd react to what came next. "You were there for me earlier."

She squeezed my arm. "I just held you."

"It was more than that. Physically, I would've crumbled without you. There's no way I could've controlled the energy without you, what did you call it, grounding me?"

She shrugged, but her eyes sparkled. "We can call it that. Scientifically, I'd like to do a little more research."

"I would too." I paused. "To see if I could direct it. Maybe even push it away when it comes."

Jo narrowed her eyes thoughtfully as if trying to read between my words. I twined my fingers in hers, trying to figure it out for myself. And I knew. I'd known for a while.

"I'd like to work on living my own life, rather than observing other people's. They get in the way of me moving forward."

Her hand tightened in mine. "Let's do it. I don't know what that would look like, but you need to move forward."

"Thank you."

"With me, I hope. I know it's ridiculous to make plans. We basically just met…" I heard a little of Lauren's prattle in her. A little more nervous and a lot more endearing. She ran a hand through her hair. "I mean, I'm over Camille, and I think you're over Keera."

I nodded emphatically.

"Thank goodness. It's hard to put yourself out there."

We both chuckled at the same time, and that solidarity sealed the deal. I was hopeful that this new relationship would work. On paper, we couldn't be more different, but sitting here on the couch, I thought we had a real shot. We looked at each other, full of hope and wonder, and Lauren barged in, breathing heavily.

She waved the final letter from Eliza's relatives. "I forgot this, so I had to go back." She came round into the room. "We'll need this for it to work."

Jo looked at me, and I shrugged. "She has a plan," I said.

"I always have a plan." Lauren motioned to the letters still spread out neatly on the coffee table. "I put them back in order of dates after I scanned them. We need to put them back the way Joelyn had them." She picked up the thick red ribbon on one edge of the table and dangled it in the air.

Without protest, Jo and I slid off the couch and sat cross-legged on the floor. Our knees touched comfortably, a small unspoken connection that neither of us pulled away from.

Little touches like this. That's how relationships are built.

Working together, we pulled the letters into a pile, pausing to reread a line or two. Since we knew the end now, each one was a new glance into their lives, a window into their love and struggles. The pile grew into a neat stack, and when we were done, Lauren slotted the letter never sent at the bottom of the pile.

"There," she said giving it a dramatic flourish.

It took three of us to tie the red ribbon. Lauren wanted it exactly as we'd found it, the ribbon crisscrossing over the letters both horizontally and vertically, finished with a Tiffany bow right in the center.

"Now the story is complete." Lauren patted the letters when they were back on the table.

As soon as her fingers brushed against the pack, the energy of the house shifted and started to gather. The low buzz I'd been feeling since we came to the den intensified, now flowing around the room, collecting over the coffee table. I reached out to grab it, but this time, I couldn't catch it.

Lauren gasped a little. "Is something happening?"

I nodded, and her eyes filled with wonder.

"I feel it," she said, closing her eyes to test her theory. When she opened them, she dug into her jeans pocket and pulled out the pendant. It swung on the chain like a diviner's pendulum, already drawn to its partner in the silver box.

"How?" Jo asked.

I shrugged, and Lauren moved where Joelyn's half of the heart pendant still lay. Jo and I rose to join her, and we all stared at Joelyn's half lying sad and alone in the silver box. The letters had never said exactly what the hearts meant to the couple, but the symbolism was clear. They had been two halves of one bond meant to fit together.

Without speaking, Jo reached into the box and picked up Joelyn's half. As it cleared the silver box, the energy continued to gather in the room, spiraling over the coffee table like a small cyclone.

I slid my arm around Jo, and she leaned close enough to let me know that she felt it too. All the while, Lauren moved the pendant closer to its other half. Her hand was steady, her movements deliberate, as though the pendants were calling to each other. The energy in the room stilled, almost as if it were holding its breath. Time itself was suspended, and the air thickened with anticipation.

When the necklaces touched, they clicked together with a quiet, satisfying certainty. I gasped as the energy transformed. What had been jagged since the moment I stepped into Meerblick began to smooth out. A spike jolted through it, and I felt…I don't know…the only way I could describe it was a gentle sigh of relief. A warm pulse of power enveloped us. The hum that had once been chaotic transformed into something steady and serene. Like the rush of seeing someone dearly loved. Not the wild, early rush but the quiet, enduring love that came with time.

All the tension I'd been holding, maybe since I picked up Lauren's frantic call, dissipated and ebbed away.

Lauren sighed deeply. "Did you feel that?"

We all laughed.

"I felt it too," Jo said, putting a hand on my knee.

"It was beautiful." Lauren clutched the united heart in one hand. "Maybe we all have a little bit of your gift, Hazel. Maybe it's buried deeper, waiting to be found."

"I really hope that's true."

"I'm going to go digging right now." Lauren was bouncing on her toes again. "Joelyn needs to know what happened. She needs to know about Eliza and her long line of daughters and how things have changed in this century." Then, she looked at us both, flashed us a quick smile, and crossed her arms. "Could I have a little privacy?"

"Absolutely," Jo said almost too fast and pulled me from the room.

Outside in the hallway, Jo shut the door. Inside, Lauren was already introducing herself to her aunt and how they were related.

"She'll be in there for hours. Lauren doesn't know how to tell a quick story."

"And she finally has the whole story and—"

I stopped midsentence because Jo was looking at me with a mixture of adoration and desire. Honestly, I'd never seen anything so wonderful.

She gently, and somehow not so gently, pushed me up against the wall and kissed me deeply. Her lips pressed firmly against mine. The kiss was full of hunger and heat, and my body arched, rising to meet hers. The physicality of her touch was new enough to send my heart racing, but there was something so comforting in it as well. Like slipping into a soft sweater on a cold day. One I could wear for a long time.

The kiss deepened and pushed all thoughts from my mind. I gave in to it. I needed to think less and do more.

"I've wanted to do that since I picked you up yesterday." She nuzzled my neck after the kiss had run its course. "And this," she said, pulling me down the hallway, "since you showed up days ago. Come on. Let's go upstairs."

"What about Lauren?" I asked, resisting only a little.

"Oh, she'll be fine."

"Joelyn can't hear her," I said, hoping that I wasn't killing whatever was going to happen next.

"I know that. And she does too. But it won't stop her."

Jo stepped closer and ran her free hand down my back. It rested on my bottom with a teasing squeeze. Then she tugged me down the hall again.

"Where are we going?"

"We're going upstairs. To my room. Where we're going to be alone together. And not to presume, but we're about to enjoy each other so much that we'll create the cleanest, most vivid reflection that this house has ever seen."

My chest fluttered in anticipation and desire. I too had wanted to be with Jo since she had told Lauren she *was taking me up to bed*. And now, she actually was.

I pulled her back teasing out this wonderful feeling. "We just got rid of the energy, and now you want to bring it back?"

"I do."

"Oh, so you're a believer now?"

"Yes, in so many things."

She turned and walked down the hall. I followed, and every step was a declaration that I was on the exact right path for me.

We reached her room, and the world faded away. Whatever memories lingered in the house, whatever energy still hummed in its bones, it fell silent as we discovered each other. What happened next was heat and connection and yes, super hot. So much so that whoever saw the reflection of our first time in the future would be forever changed by it. It changed me too.

Creating reflections, the good kind, was so much better than observing them.

THE JOURNAL

The Past: Joelyn

Love is forever.

My hand strokes your thigh. You moan, and goose bumps rise across your skin. I move closer to your center, your legs instinctively part. With swirling caresses, my hand inches upward. At the threshold of our deepest intimacy, the softest place of you, where I want to be more than any place in the world, I freeze. Is it too much? Do you want this as much as I do? My hand hovers over you, and then, as if sensing my doubt, you grab my hand and guide it home. On you. In you. I find your rhythm. You move with me, rising and falling in perfect sync. I am the moon, and you are the tide answering my pull. You call out my name. It's music, something holy and wild and new, that I have never heard before. A song that resonates with my soul. Higher and higher, you climb. I can see you are on the verge of ecstasy. Your body trembles. It tenses with a hard contraction and explodes around my fingers. Raw. Beautiful. Transcendent. The energy we have created surges with a blinding light into the room. It will remain here long after us. Energy is forever.

Love is Forever

EPILOGUE

The Present: Hazel

Lauren stood in the center of the Blue Room on a blustery fall day, holding up an embossed silver shadow box. The dozen guests peered in for a better look. "Love is forever, and it has brought everyone in the room together. So may I present to you Joelyn and Eliza, who found true love and each other right here in this room."

The frame gleamed in the soft afternoon light. Embossed along its edge were two women under palm trees. Lauren had designed it herself to echo the silver box from the wall. Inside, there was the simple handwritten letter from Eliza. *Yes. I love you too.* With the ornate loops and curls, the letter was practically a work of art itself. The sentiment certainly was.

Beside it were delicately painted flowers, the united pendants—minus their chains—and the only picture of the couple on the beach. Lauren had zoomed in on the two of them, cropping everyone else so only Joelyn and Eliza stared at us from the past. She had done a great job.

The room had also been transformed: huge bouquets of trailing jasmine vines combined with fluffy peonies, garden roses, and hydrangea. The all-white arrangements popped against the blue walls, and their scent infused the air with a delicate floral fragrance. Making no bones about it, Lauren was throwing a wedding. Champagne chilled in silver buckets, and downstairs, a vanilla and berry cake with two brides as the cake topper sat on a sideboard. Every detail was deliberate, thoughtful, and unapologetically over-the-top.

On the wall, long repaired thanks to Leo, a hook hung right over the spot where we'd found Joelyn's box in the summer. With *Canon in D* playing softly in the background, Lauren stepped up to the wall. "May some of their love live here forever."

She hung the shadow box on the hook, and the room erupted into applause.

"It will," I said. "This is amazing, Lauren."

Lauren beamed as *congratulations* and *great jobs* were heaped upon her.

"I had to stop her from using real gold leaf on the flowers," Jo whispered beside me, her breath warm and soft against my ear.

"Stop it. You're terrible." I pinched her side. "Don't tease Lauren on her big day."

"You want terrible? Pinch me lower next time."

I swatted her arm, suppressing my laughter.

"What's going on over there?" Gran asked from the other side of the room.

Jo and I giggled but straightened like a couple of schoolgirls in front of the headmistress. Shaking her head, Gran turned back to her conversation with Jo's mother, who had flown in from France ostensibly for the ceremony but mostly to meet me. Thankfully, it was going well.

Around the room, the eclectic group laughed with good cheer. Leo stood near the door talking with Lauren's parents while Maggie and Lynn circled the room. Lynn's husband, Tom, a little baffled by the ceremony, was putting on a brave face. He, as it turned out, was an architect and had fallen in love with Meerblick at first glance. So lots of love was in the air.

"This house has incredible energy," Tom said for what must have been the third time. "I'd love to know how the original architect managed it."

Across the room, I smiled and said nothing.

Lynn's teenage daughters had thrown themselves into Lauren's vision with gusto, playing flower girls for the day. They'd even woven matching flowers into Edgar's collar. He took everything with his usual good nature and sat in the middle of things, looking happily from person to person.

The ceremony was kitschy, ridiculous, and absolutely perfect. And somehow, it was also a celebration of all the magnificent turns my life had taken in the past few months. Jo and I had moved from that tumultuous beginning to an easy, ever deepening relationship. She had taken a job in the Berkeley plasma lab and, bit by bit, had been bringing her things from her aunt's house to my condo. The day that she'd showed up with a bed for Edgar, I knew we were on the road to something really special.

I wasn't the only one who saw it. Gran had embraced Jo into our family with arms she had never opened for Keera. On quiet nights, the two of them could be found rocking on Gran's porch in matching rockers, drinking tea, and theorizing about my gift. Together, through trial and error, they'd devised exercises that finally allowed me to block the energy and the reflections when I didn't want them.

Maybe it was Jo, maybe it was learning to live my own life instead of constantly stepping into the lives of others. Whatever the reason, I was more energized and less drained. Generally, my edges were smoother and my foundation stronger.

And my professional life was on an even keel for the first time ever. I'd stopped trying to be the artist I wasn't and completely embraced the artist I was. My artwork had never been better, and the new otter show was a runaway success. Lana had been a huge part of that, her enthusiasm and sharp eye breathing new life into the gallery. I told her every day that we were lucky to have her.

Even Keera had come around in her own way. She'd met almost every demand that my lawyer proposed, except for the crazy ones Kenning had tossed in for bait negotiation. We forged a contract that was clear, fair, and more importantly, manageable. We were about to head out on the live mascot shoot now that she had worked her magic, and the college football season was in full swing. She had even thanked me for reaching out to my contacts for Cherry. She had found some catalog work and was appreciative, though not enough to tell me herself. Keera, however, was legitimately grateful enough for them both.

The pop of the champagne cork brought me back to the moment. Lauren and Tom were making the rounds, filling glasses, and the room buzzed with laughter and toasts to love.

As I clinked glasses with Jo, I felt the familiar tug of the house's energy brushing at my mind. It had been silent since the day we'd united the necklaces in the den, as if it had finally settled. But now, for obvious reasons, it was stirring again.

Instead of shutting it out, I let it in. The energy flowed easily, creating a connection, and a reflection shimmered to life.

Jo and Eliza dressed in their nightclothes also now stood in the center of the room. Since this imprint had two people in it, I guessed my hard work was paying off. As soon as they appeared, everyone subconsciously edged away, and so from my perspective, they looked like they had joined us in the celebration.

Joelyn lovingly cupped the back of Eliza's neck, her fingers threading through Eliza's hair. Eliza arched, her body melting with trust and love.

I laughed softly. Jo, who must've sensed something, slipped her hand into mine, her grip grounding me as usual. The reflection sharpened. Edgar whipped his head around and was riveted to the couple. His tail thumped happily on the floor.

Joelyn bent, pressing kisses to each of Eliza's closed eyes. Her face softened as if every worry dissolved under Joelyn's touch.

"To the happy couple," someone called as another champagne bottle popped.

As if Joelyn and Eliza had heard the toast, Joelyn smiled. She leaned in, brushing her lips gently against Eliza's. The kiss deepened, so full of tenderness and love, it could've been the culmination of a real wedding ceremony.

Delighted, I laughed, the sound fizzing up like the champagne bubbles in my glass.

I turned to find Jo staring at me with a look mirroring Joelyn's. My breath caught, and for a moment, the world narrowed to only us two. I fell into that gaze and let the energy go. The reflection faded in my peripheral vision. Everything I wanted, everything I needed, was right here in the present with Jo.

Her eyes sparkled with something deeper than happiness, a quiet knowing that sent shivers to my toes.

"Let's toast to love. All kinds. Even the messy, uncontrollable kind." Jo's lips curved into a smile.

The words tumbled out of me, unbidden and raw. "I love you." I surprised myself. We'd never said it before, even if we'd shown it in a million different ways. The rush of emotion, the reflection, her closeness threw me headlong into the romantic moment. I'd struggled hard over the last few months to gain control of my life. With these three little words, I'd given it right back. I'd opened myself up to losing control all over again.

"Yes. I love you too." Her response hit me like the sweetest avalanche.

She had used the words from the letter, consciously or subconsciously.

I didn't ask.

It didn't matter.

Control, as it turned out, was way overrated.

About the Author

Catherine Lane started to write fiction on a dare from her wife. She's thrilled to be a published author and happily admits her wife was right. They live in Southern California with their son and a very mischievous rescue dog.

Catherine spends most of her time teaching, mothering, or writing. But when she finds herself at loose ends, she enjoys experimenting with soup recipes in the kitchen, paddling her kayak on long stretches of flat water, and trying, unsuccessfully, to outwit her dog.

Books Available From Bold Strokes Books

Anywhere with You by Margo Glynn. On a road trip through the Great American Southwest, two friends discover nature, hope, and each other. (978-1-63679-907-0)

Burning Bridges by Lesley Davis. Can Clancy and Jude crack the case of eight missing women—and the secrets of their own hearts? (978-1-63679-872-1)

Dreams Entangled by Sophia Kell Hagin. Amid self-doubt, secrets, a pandemic, fear of attack and attempted murder, Pirin and Gracie's attraction turns to love, and their lives will never be the same. (978-1-63679-892-9)

Echoes of Love by Catherine Lane. As Hazel's and Jo's paths intertwine, they're swept up in a whirlwind of long-buried secrets, sizzling chemistry, and memories that won't be denied. (978-1-63679-835-6)

The Fame Game by Ronica Black. Wild child Hollywood actress Luna Kirkman begins dating Hollywood's leading man, only to fall for his straitlaced sister instead. (978-1-63679-858-5)

Moonlight Obsession by Sheri Lewis Wohl. All it takes to stop a clever killer is moonlight, love, and a silver bullet. (978-1-63679-831-8)

My Boyfriend's Wife by Joy Argento. Amid betrayal and heartbreak, can two women discover a love that could heal their pasts and rewrite their futures? (978-1-63679-866-0)

Tapout by Nicole Disney. A struggling MMA fighter finds her edge in an underground ring, but as she falls for the magnetic and ambitious promoter behind the matches, their dangerous world threatens to destroy everything they've fought to rebuild. (978-1-63679-924-7)

An Extraordinary Passion by Kit Meredith. An autistic podcaster must decide whether to take a chance on her polyamorous guest and indulge their shared passion, despite her history. (978-1-63679-679-6)

Heart's Appraisal by Jo Hemmingwood. Andy and Hazel can't deny their attraction, but they'll never agree on the place they call home. (978-1-63679-856-1)

That's Amore by Georgia Beers. The romantic city of Rome should inspire Lily's passion for writing, if she can look away from Marina Troiani, her witty, smart, and unassumingly beautiful Italian tour guide. (978-1-63679-841-7)

Through Sky and Stars by Tessa Croft. Can Val and Nicole's love cross space and time to change the fate of humanity? (978-1-63679-862-2)

Uncomplicate It by Kel McCord. When an office attraction threatens her career, Hollis Reed's carefully laid plans demand revision. (978-1-63679-864-6)

The Unexpected Heiress by Cassidy Crane. When a cynical opportunist meets a shy but spirited heiress, the last thing she plans is for her heart to get involved. (978-1-63679-833-2)

Vanguard by Gun Brooke. Beth Wild, Subterranean freedom fighter, is in the crosshairs when she fights for her people and risks her heart for loving the exacting Celestial dissident leader, LaSierra Delmonte. (978-1-63679-818-9)

Wild Night Rising by Barbara Ann Wright. Riding Harleys instead of horses, the Wild Hunt of myth is once again unleashed upon the world. Their ousted leader and a fey cop must join forces to rein in the ride of terror. (978-1-63679-749-6)

A Thousand Tiny Promises by Morgan Lee Miller. When estranged childhood friends Audrey and Reid reunite to fulfill their best friend's dying wish, the last thing they expect is a journey toward healing their broken friendship and discovering a newfound love for each other. (978-1-63679-630-7)

Behold My Heart by Ronica Black. Alora Anders is a highly successful artist who's losing her vision. Devastated, she hires Bodie Banks, a young struggling sculptor, as a live-in assistant. Can Alora open her mind and her heart to accept Bodie into her life? (978-1-63679-810-3)

Fearless Hearts by Radclyffe. One wounded woman, one determined to protect her—and a summertime of risk, danger, and desire. (978-1-63679-837-0)